THE LANGOLIERS

adapted for the screen by

TOM HOLLAND

Encyclopocalypse Publications
www.encyclopocalypse.com

PART 1

ACT 1

EXT. LOS ANGELES INTERNATIONAL AIRPORT - NIGHT

The place is a madhouse. People arrive and leave, cars honking as they try to get in and out.

CREDITS ROLL

EXT. PARKING LOT - NIGHT

Jammed with cars, people hurrying to and fro from the terminal.

INT. FORD TAURUS - NIGHT

NICK HOPEWELL, late 30s, sits on the passenger side of the front seat, staring at the picture of a very pretty young woman. He wears horn-rimmed glasses, a starched dress shirt, and jeans. He slides the photo back into its envelope and turns to the hard-faced man next to him, HARKER, 50.

> NICK
> She`s just an innocent
> bystander.

> HARKER
> So what`s new.

> NICK
> Tell them I won`t do it.

He tosses the envelope on the seat between them and reaches for the door. Harker grabs him.

> HARKER
> It has to be done by next Thursday. And make sure it`s in Boston where he lives.

Their eyes meet and hold. A beat. Then Nick tears free and leaps out, slamming the door behind him and walking for the terminal. Harker yells after him.

> HARKER
> See you in London on Saturday! We`ll have a pint!

Nick continues on without a backward glance.

EXT. CURB SIDE CHECK-IN - DAY

Nick crosses in back of two women at the curb side check-in, and disappears into the terminal. AUNT VICKI, pleasant looking, 40 plus, talks to the attendant while her niece, DINAH BELLMAN, stands alongside. Dinah is 12 and blind. She wears dark glasses with pink bows and a pink travel dress to match.

> AUNT VICKI
> That`s right. Flight 29 to Boston --

Behind them a limo pulls to a halt and CRAIG TOOMY steps out.

He is a bland looking businessman in his early 30s. He carries a briefcase and hand luggage. He makes his way for the door as a cab screeches to halt behind him and RICHARD LOGAN, late 20s, leaps out. He sees Toomy and starts yelling wildly.

                    LOGAN
          Mr. Toomy! Mr. Toomy --

Toomy stops and turns back as Logan hurries up to him. By the check-in counter, Dinah turns blindly in their direction, her attention caught by the shouting. Logan stops before Toomy, waving a sheaf of computer printouts.

                    LOGAN
                  (continuing)
          Thank God, I caught
          you. I checked over the
          figures on those foreign
          bonds you bought and
          you`ve _lost_ money, not
          made it.

Toomy looks at him, smiling pleasantly, almost as if he hadn`t heard him.

                    TOOMY
          Really? Did you check
          my hotel reservation? I
          wanted a corner suite,
          remember?

Logan stares at him disbelievingly, not understanding his reaction.

                    LOGAN
          Mr. Toomy, did you hear
          what I just said? <u>You`ve
          lost forty-three million
          dollars.</u>

Toomy snaps out of it, changing gears without missing a beat, suddenly acting very concerned.

                    TOOMY
          What? There must be a
          mistake --

He grabs the computer printouts, scanning them as Logan anxiously watches.

                    LOGAN
          I checked and rechecked,
          but couldn`t find any --

Toomy pockets the computer printouts.

                    TOOMY
          I`ll study them on the
          plane to Boston.

                    LOGAN
          But, Mr. Toomy, you`re
          supposed to meet with the
          board of directors. What
          are you going to tell
          them?

                    TOOMY
          Why, the truth, of course.
          And stop worrying.
          I`m sure it`s just a
          mathematical error.

With that he turns and continues into the
terminal, Logan staring after him. Near
the outside check-in stand, Dinah follows
Mr. Toomy with her blind eyes, almost as
though she can psychically sense him.
Finished checking the baggage, Aunt Vicki
turns to her niece.

                  AUNT VICKI
          Ready to go, dear.

Dinah nods after Toomy.

                    DINAH
          Something`s wrong inside
          that man`s head. His
          thoughts --

                  AUNT VICKI
          Oh, Dinah, don`t start
          that again.

Grasping the girl`s hand, she pulls her
toward the terminal.

INT. TERMINAL CAUSEWAY - DAY

Toomy passes through security and walks
down the causeway, <u>casually discarding
the printouts in a trash can</u> as he passes
two women lost in conversation against the

wall. One is DORIS HEARTMAN, a motor mouth housewife in her 30s, the other, LAUREL STEVENSON, a pretty, light-haired woman, also in her 30s.

                    DORIS
          Now that I`ve given you a
          lift to the airport, do
          you want to tell me why
          you`re going to Boston?

Laurel smiles at her.

                    LAUREL
          Doris, stop that. It`s
          none of your business and
          you know it.

                    DORIS
          I know, but this is just
          so unlike you. Flying off
          to a strange city for no
          reason and not telling
          your best friend why --

The P.A. system suddenly interrupts her as Nick passes through security behind them, walking down the corridor.

                    P.A. SYSTEM (OVER)
          Flight 29 at Gate Three
          will begin immediate
          boarding for Boston.

Laurel seizes on it as an excuse for getting out of there.

                    LAUREL
          Oh, gosh, there`s my
          flight. Gotta go, Doris.
          Thanks loads.

She gives her a big hug and turns for the
boarding area only to run smack into Nick
who is just passing. Her purse falls to
the ground and she reaches for it.

                    LAUREL
          Oh, excuse me --

Nick reaches down, beating her to the
purse. He rises, handing it to her with a
smile.

                    NICK
          Perfectly all right.

He heads on for the boarding area as Laurel
exchanges a wave with Doris and hurries
after him.

EXT. RUNWAY - NIGHT

A long white L1011 passenger jet touches
down, bouncing once before it hugs the
runway. Along the fuselage, "AMERICAN
PRIDE" is written in letters raked backward
to indicate speed. The plane slows and
taxis for the jet ways.

EXT. TERMINAL - NIGHT

The screaming jet engines cut off and the

huge airplane rolls to a silent stop in front of the boarding dock.

INT. COCKPIT - NIGHT

The pilot, BRIAN ENGLE, a pleasant looking man in his 40s, shuts down the jets and switches to AP (auxiliary power). He leans over his control board with a frown, checking a gauge that reads CABIN PRESSURE.

                    BRIAN
          Damn. This gauge doesn`t
          tell me anything. The
          leak could have been
          anywhere.

He sits back with an exhausted sigh as his co-pilot, DANNY KEENE, mid-30`s, watches him.

                    DANNY
          Don`t worry about it.
          They don`t like it, but
          it`s diagnostic`s problem
          now.

                    BRIAN
          I don`t care what they
          like and what they don`t.
          You know what a pressure
          blow-out can do. We were
          all damn near human pate.

Danny nods. He knows. Outside the windows, the boarding ramp slides into place and they hear the forward door open and passengers begin to disembark. Brian rubs his forehead. Strain has given him a whammer of a headache.

> **BRIAN**
> I don`t know. Maybe I`m getting too old for this business.

There is a sudden knock on the door and STEVE SEARLES, the navigator, 30, turns in his seat at the back of the cockpit, opening it without rising.

JAMES DEEGAN stands there, 50 plus, the name tag on his American Pride blazer identifying him as Deputy Chief of Operations for the airline at LAX. He looks at Brian.

> **DEEGAN**
> Captain Engle?

Brian stares up at him defensively.

> **BRIAN**
> Yes, but I don`t know what to tell you. We couldn`t find the pressure leak.

> **DEEGAN**
> This isn`t about the leak, Captain. Could I talk to you outside, please.

Alarm sweeps Brian`s face.

                    BRIAN
          Why? What`s wrong?

                    DEEGAN
          Outside, please.

He disappears from the doorway. Brian
exchanges a helpless look with his co-
pilot and navigator, grabs his overnight
bag from the back shelf, and follows Deegan
out of the cockpit.

INT. JETWAY - NIGHT

Brian joins Deegan, the two men walking
up the jetway with the flow of debarking
passengers.

                    BRIAN
          You want to tell me
          what`s going on?

                    DEEGAN
          It`s about your wife.

Brian looks at him blankly.

                    BRIAN
          My wife? Oh, you mean my
          ex-wife. We`re divorced.
          Why, what about her?

                    DEEGAN
          There`s been an accident.
          Perhaps you`d better come
          up to my office

Brian stops, staring at the man. Foreboding sweeps him. Whatever this is, he just knows it is going to make the pressure leak pale by comparison.

                    BRIAN
          What about Annie? How
          badly has she been hurt?

Nothing from Deegan. Brian's foreboding turns to certainty.

                    BRIAN
          Is she dead?

Deegan looks away, hating this. He finally nods.

                    DEEGAN
          Yes -- I'm afraid she is.
          There was a fire in her
          apartment. The family's
          asked that you come back
          for the funeral.

Brian nods numbly, staring at nothing. Deegan watches him, concerned.

                    DEEGAN
          Are you all right,
          Captain?

Brian snaps out of it, a little bit.

                    BRIAN
          Yes, it's just a shock,
          that's all.

Deegan glances at his watch.

> DEEGAN
> There`s a red-eye leaving
> for Boston right now. You
> can dead head back on it
> if you want?

> BRIAN
> Yes. I guess I`d better.

The two men continue up the jetway.

INT. BOARDING ROTUNDA - NIGHT

Brian and Deegan emerge through the
boarding door with the other deplaning
passengers. They cut across the rotunda
for Gate 3. The electronic boarding sign
above the check-in desk reads AMERICAN
PRIDE FLIGHT 27: LAX TO BOSTON, IMMEDIATE
BOARDING.

The other gate areas are relatively empty,
but this one is crowded with well over two
hundred passengers.

Deegan nods in their direction as they
skirt the perimeter, headed for the jetway.

> DEEGAN
> Looks like a full flight.

> BRIAN
> I guess. What`s the
> weather like?

                    DEEGAN
          Clouds at 20,000 feet
          from the Great Plains all
          the way to Boston. Oh,
          and we`ve had reports of
          the Aurora Borealis over
          the Mojave Desert.

                    BRIAN
          Northern lights over
          California? At this time
          of year?

Deegan shrugs.

                    DEEGAN
          Who knows? The weather
          has been really freaky
          lately.

They slip around the GATE AGENT who
is taking tickets from the boarding
passengers. Craig Toomy is holding up the
line as he argues with the agent.

                    TOOMY
          I asked for a window seat
          and I want a window seat.

The agent smiles, trying to be pleasant as
she watches the line grow behind Toomy.

Directly behind him stands Laurel
Stevenson, waiting patiently, ticket in
hand, and behind her, Nick Hopewell,
tapping his foot with equal impatience.
Behind them, farther down the line, are

Aunt Vicki and Dinah.

                    AGENT
          Of course, sir. Why don`t
          you talk to the ticketing
          agent

                    TOOMY
          I don`t want to talk to
          the ticketing agent. I
          want to talk to you.

Brian and Deegan slip past and disappear
down the boarding ramp.

INT. JETWAY BOARDING RAMP - NIGHT

Deegan nods back over his shoulder as they
walk, referring to Toomy.

                    DEEGAN
            There`s one on every
            flight, isn`t there?

                    BRIAN
          Always.

They come to a stop just outside the door
of the plane. Deegan turns to Brian.

                    DEEGAN
          Have a good trip, Captain,
          and my condolences.

                    BRIAN
          Thank you.

The two men shake and Brian disappears into the plane as Deegan starts the walk back up the jetway, passing Toomy and the others hurrying for their seats.

EXT. LAX RUNWAY - TWENTY MINUTES LATER

American Pride Flight 29, a Boeing 767, accelerates down the runway and becomes airborne, disappearing upward into the darkness and clouds.

INT. FLIGHT 29 - NIGHT

Brian watches as the seat belt sign flashes off and unbuckles himself. He grabs a pillow and blanket from the empty seat next to him, trying to make himself comfortable. First class is half full, but the main cabin behind him is jammed. He puts his seat back all the way down, scrunches up and closes his eyes. He quickly drifts off to sleep.

(CREDITS END)

EXT. SKY - NIGHT -LATER

The 767 cruises gracefully through the night sky. It looks so peaceful you`d never know a thing was wrong.

INT. MAIN CABIN - COACH CLASS SECTION - NIGHT

Dinah Bellman slowly wakes, stretching

with a yawn. She turns to the seat next to her.

                    DINAH
          Aunt Vicki, could I have
          a glass of water, please?

No reply. Thinking her aunt must be asleep, Dinah reaches out to touch her.

                    DINAH
          Aunt Vicki

But her hand touches air. Her aunt is not there. She feels the seat next to her, and finds a Romance novel her aunt was reading when she fell asleep. It doesn`t reassure her. She keeps feeling about the seat only to find her aunt`s purse. This alarms her even more. She knows her aunt wouldn`t leave her seat without it. She lifts her head, cocking an ear, expecting to hear the sounds of life around her, a few passengers murmuring among themselves, the clink of glasses, a hollow cough. Instead all she hears is the steady drone of the jets. And nothing else.

Controlling her growing panic, Dinah fumbles for the controls beside the seat. The reading light above her flashes on and off as she punches the buttons, searching for the one that summonses the stewardess. She finally finds it and hears a faint chime as the bell goes off. She relaxes, expecting the flight attendant to be there any moment. Only she doesn`t come. Dinah rings the call button again. The chime sounds once more, but it is the only sound in the cabin except for the soft drone of the jets. She stands, looking blindly about as she calls out.

>   DINAH
>   Would somebody speak to
>   me, please. I`m sorry,
>   but my aunt is gone and
>   I`m blind.

No answer. Trying to contain her rising panic, she steps forward to the next row, leaning down, touching the bottom of the starboard side seat. It is empty, completely empty. She straightens, calling out again, her voice louder this time.

>   DINAH
>   Hello? Is anybody here?
>   <u>Anybody!</u>

Still no answer. She steps forward to the next row, leans down, her arms outstretched, her fingers splayed, feeling the seat. She touches another purse, a briefcase, and a pad and pencil. But the seat itself is also empty. She moves to the next row, murmuring to herself in barely controlled panic.

>   DINAH
>   Dear God, let somebody be
>   here, please. Anybody,
>   anybody at all!

She continues down the aisle, missing ALBERT KAUSSNER two seats away in the middle section. He is a gawky 18 year old in a pair of baggy jeans and a Hard Rock Cafe t-shirt. He is sound asleep. Dinah comes to a stop several rows down, and leans forward, touching the seat to the port side. She feels a pair of earphones lying there as though dropped unexpectedly. Then her hand closes around something shaggy and strange feeling. She lifts it and although she cannot see it, she can feel it. Hair! Somebody`s been scalped! She drops it, stumbling back with an ear-piercing scream.

                    DINAH
          Nooooooo!!!!

INT. FIRST CLASS SECTION - NIGHT

Dinah`s scream snaps Brian awake and brings him to his feet. He dives toward the curtain that separates First from Business Class. He passes a sleeping Craig Toomy on his way. He is moving so fast it does not register on him that except for himself, Toomy is the only other person in the first class section.

INT. BUSINESS SECTION - NIGHT

Brian comes through the curtain, only dimly aware that there are only two people in Business Class, both sleeping, a bald headed man in a three-piece brown suit, and Nick Hopewell. Nick wakes as Brian races past toward the curtain that hides the main cabin.

INT. COACH SECTION - NIGHT

He bursts through the curtain to see the source of the screaming, Dinah, several rows ahead, her pink dress flowing, her dark eye glasses askew, her outstretched hands feeling blindly about her. Brian grabs her, trying to calm her, speaking softly so as not to wake the other passengers.

> BRIAN
>> It`s all right, kid.
>> What`s wrong?

Dinah latches on to him frantically.

> DINAH
>> Where is everybody?
>> They`ve gone, they`ve all
>> gone!

> BRIAN
>> What do you mean? Where`s
>> everybody

He looks up, the words dying on his lips as he sees what Dinah is talking about. <u>Except for themselves, there is apparently no one else in the vast cabin of over two hundred seats</u>. It is completely, totally deserted. Suddenly Albert Kaussner stands in the center row of seats, blinking owlishly at Brian and Dinah as he, too, looks about the rows of empty seats with stunned disbelief. He turns his gaze on Brian and the girl.

                    ALBERT
          What happened? Did we
          land while I was asleep
          and let the others off?

Brian can only look at him and shrug helplessly. Dinah begins to sob, panic welling up inside her like a huge tidal wave.

                    DINAH
          My Aunt Vicki`s gone!
          Where`s my aunt? Please,
          I want my aunt!

Brian snaps out of his shock, and turns his attention to her.

                    BRIAN
          You`re all right, young
          lady. What`s your name?

                    DINAH
          Dinah. I can`t find my
          aunt. I`m blind and I
          can`t see her. I woke up
          and her seat was empty --

DON GAFFNEY, a large man in his late 40s, slowly rises out of a seat in the middle row toward the back. He wears a red flannel shirt and looks utterly bewildered. His gaze is fixed on Brian.

GAFFNEY
Who`s screaming? Is the
plane in trouble, mister?

Before Brian can answer, another man, BOB
JENKINS, rises out of his seat, blinking
sleepily. He is 60 plus, has white tufts
of hair going every which way, and wears
a ratty plaid sport coat. Laurel slowly
rises up out of her seat on the port side,
looking at them. Jenkins stares around
with mute but alert curiosity while Laurel
rubs sleep out of her eyes, looking at all
the empty seats in a stunned, disoriented
way.

LAUREL
Where is everybody?

Farther up along the port side an attractive
young girl of 17, BETHANY SIMMS, stands.

She stretches, stifling a yawn, and looks
at the others with a slightly stoned gaze.

BETHANY
What`s going on? Are we
in Boston already?

Nobody answers as Craig Toomy appears
through the curtain behind Brian. Behind
him is Nick, pulling his spectacles and
putting them on.

Toomy is the first to speak, nodding toward
the sobbing Dinah impatiently.

                    TOOMY
          What`s going on? Can`t
          somebody shut that brat
          up?

Brian ignores him, concentrating on Dinah.

                    BRIAN
          You`re not alone. There
          are other people here.
          Can you hear them?

She nods, stifling the tears.

                    DINAH
          Y-yes. I can hear them.
          But where`s Aunt Vicki?
          And who`s been killed?

Laurel looks at her sharply, her face
filling with dread.

                    LAUREL
          Killed? Has someone been
          killed? Have we been
          hijacked?

                    BRIAN
          No one`s been killed.

He looks around, still trying to get his
bearings. Dinah chimes in insistently.

                    DINAH
          I felt his hair. Someone
          cut off his HAIR!

Brian turns to silently count the passengers. Dinah, Albert, Craig Toomy, Laurel, Bethany, Bob Jenkins, Nick Hopewell, and Don Gaffney. That, plus the bald-headed man still sleeping in Business Class, makes -- but Nick steps up to him, speaking before Brian can finish his count.

                    NICK
          Ten counting yourself
          and the guy still asleep
          in Business Class. What
          about crew? Anybody know
          about them?

                    BRIAN
          Not yet, but I was just
          about to find out.

Brian looks at the man in the red flannel shirt, Don Gaffney, and nods at Dinah.

                    BRIAN
          I have to go forward.
          Stay with the little
          girl.

                    GAFFNEY
          All right, but what`s
          happening?

Brian ignores the question, walking toward the front of the plane.

The others stare after him, for the moment still too stunned to move.

INT. FIRST CLASS SERVICE AREA - NIGHT

Brian comes to a halt behind the movie screen and between the two first-class heads. The area is empty. He pokes his head into the galley. Empty also, but Brian sees the beverage trolley parked halfway down the opposite aisle. Used glasses from the pre-takeoff drink dot the bottom shelf. He heads for the cockpit door. He knocks. No answer. He visibly pales as he curls his fingers into a fist and pounds on the door.

                    BRIAN
          Hello, you guys! Open the
          door!

INT. MAIN CABIN -COACH CLASS - NIGHT

The small group huddles together. Craig Toomy keeps his distance, standing near the bulkhead to Business Class, watching the others with suspicious eyes. Laurel looks at Don Gaffney.

                    LAUREL
          What do you think
          happened? Do you think we
          landed and let the other
          passengers off?

                    GAFFNEY
          I don`t know. I was
          asleep.

Dinah turns, looking blindly in Laurel`s

direction.

                    DINAH
          You`re a teacher, aren`t
          you?

                    LAUREL
          That`s right, honey. The
          fifth grade. How did you
          know?

Dinah fumbles for her hand. She finds it
and holds on tight.

                    DINAH
          It`s in your voice. Miss
          Lee, my teacher at the
          blind school, sounds just
          like you.

                    LAUREL
          What`s your name?

Dinah looks blindly in her direction.

                    DINAH
          Dinah. Dinah Bellman.
          What`s yours?

                    LAUREL
          Laurel Stevenson.

                    DINAH
          Laurel? That`s the name
          of a flower, isn`t it?

Nick suddenly breaks in.

                    NICK
          Pardon me, but I`m going
          forward to join our
          friend.

Craig Toomy watches them, speaking in a
high-pitched voice, his face dead pale
except for a splotch of red in either
cheek.

                    TOOMY
          I want to know what`s
          going on here! I want
          to know what`s going on
          right now!

Nick shoots him a dry glance as he passes.

                    NICK
          Nor am I a bit surprised.

He disappears forward, leaving Toomy and
Gaffney standing there. Bob Jenkins, the
elderly gentleman in the frayed sport coat,
goes to the starboard window and peers
out. Laurel looks at him questioningly.

                    LAUREL
          What do you see?

Jenkins presses closer to the window,
staring down.

EXT. PLANE - NIGHT

Far below the plane, mountains can be
seen, unending ridges of them, running

diagonally like a human vertebrae, cloaked in darkness.

INT. COACH CLASS SECTION - NIGHT

Jenkins pulls his head back, looking at Laurel.

                    BOB
          Darkness and mountains.

Albert comes alive, chiming in.

                    ALBERT
          The Rockies?

                    BOB
          I believe so, young man.

Jenkins slips into the seat, bent over his clasped hands, already lost in thought. Albert turns and wanders up the aisle toward the back of the plane as Laurel sits with Dinah.

INT. FIRST CLASS - NIGHT

Brian stands in front of the locked door to the cockpit, his head bent, thinking furiously. A voice suddenly speaks from behind him.

                    NICK (O.S.)
          What`s wrong. The flight
          crew gone along with
          everybody else?

Brian looks up sharply to find himself
staring at Nick.

                    BRIAN
          I don`t know, but they
          won`t answer my calls and
          the door`s locked from
          the inside.

                    NICK
          I was afraid of that.
          Sorry to get your wind
          up. Nick Hopewell.

The two men shake, Nick studying Brian`s
uniform carefully.

                    NICK
          I am praying, sir, that
          the pilot`s cap I noticed
          on one of the first class
          seats belongs to you.

                    BRIAN
          It does. Captain
          Engle, but under the
          circumstances you can
          call me Brian.

                    NICK
          I`ll call you savior
          instead if we find what I
          expect on the other side
          of that door. But first,
          let`s see if we can get
          it open.

Nick kneels, investigating the lock to the door.

INT. COACH CABIN - NIGHT

Albert stops, lifting a hank of hair from a seat. He turns, holding it up to Dinah where she sits with Laurel.

                    ALBERT
          It`s hair you felt. I
          just found that a wig,
          not a human scalp.

Laurel turns to Dinah.

                    LAUREL
          Well, that`s a relief,
          isn`t it?

Dinah says nothing, just nestles closer to Laurel. Bob Jenkins, however, hefts himself up from his seat and joins Albert.

                    BOB
          Now why would somebody
          disappear and leave
          their hairpiece? Quite a
          mystery, don`t you think?

Albert shrugs, not knowing what to think. The two men continue down the aisle a few rows only to stop and stare, their brows slowly puckering in mutual amazement.

On the seat to one side lies a purse and what looks like a plain gold wedding ring.

Albert picks it up, he and Bob examining it silently for a moment before Albert replaces it and they continue their walk, their amazement slowly growing.

Wherever they look, they see jewelry on almost every seat, mostly wedding rings, but also diamonds, emeralds, and rubies. There are earrings, most of them five-and-dime stuff, but some of which looks very expensive indeed. There are also studs, necklaces, laptop computers, cuff links, ID bracelets, and watches, watches, watches! From Timex to Rolex, there are at least two hundred of them, lying on seats, lying on the floor in between seats, and lying in the aisles. They twinkle in the overhead lights. Bob whistles softly under his breath.

                    BOB
        My God

Albert can only nod.

                  ALBERT
        Yeah. You`re not kidding.

They continue on, the bizarre booty in the chairs and on the floor growing. There are also at least sixty pair of spectacles, wire-rimmed, horn-rimmed, gold-rimmed. There are prim glasses, punkie glasses, and glasses with rhinestones set in the bows.

There are belt buckles and service pins

and piles of pocket change. No bills, but easily four hundred dollars in quarters, dimes, nickels, and pennies. There are wallets, not as many as purses, but still a good dozen of them, from plastic to leather. There are pocket knives and almost two dozen hand-held calculators.

And odder things as well. Sparkling things, mainly silver, but some gold. Albert picks one up, holding it up to the light. It looks very much like part of a human tooth. Bob Jenkins comes up behind him, staring at it with bad eyes.

> BOB
> A silver filling, I
> think.

> ALBERT
> Yeah. I was afraid of
> that.

He drops it back in the seat gingerly, he and Jenkins looking around at all the sparkling bits of silver and gold.

Bob finally speaks in a voice tinged with more than just a little fear.

> BOB
> What the hell is going on
> here?

Behind them, Craig Toomy abruptly turns, disappearing into first class. Don Gaffney follows him.

INT. FIRST-CLASS CABIN - NIGHT

Nick is rattling the door, seeing if he can
find a simple way to force the lock. Brian
watches as Craig Toomy and Don Gaffney
appear down the aisle. They stop before
them.

Toomy stares belligerently at Brian,
addressing him in a loud voice.

                    TOOMY
          I demand to know just
          what is going on here!

Nick steps in front of Brian, answering
before the pilot can get his mouth open.

                    NICK
          Currently? We`re just
          about to break the lock
          on this door. The flight
          crew appears to have
          abdicated along with
          everybody else, but we`re
          in luck just the same.

He nods at Brian.

                    NICK
          My new acquaintance here
          just happens to be a
          pilot --

Toomy ignores Nick, sticks his face into
Brian`s, as aggressively as a ball player
disputing an empire`s call.

                    TOOMY
          Do you work for American
          Pride, friend?

                    BRIAN
          Yes, I do, but what`s
          important right now is
          that we --

                    TOOMY
          I`ll tell you what`s
          important! I`ve got a
          meeting at Boston`s
          Prudential Center at nine
          o`clock this morning.
          Promptly at nine o`clock!
          I booked a seat on this
          conveyance in good faith,
          and I have no intention
          of being late for my
          appointment! Do you
          hear me? No intention
          whatsoever!

Brian stares at the man in stunned silence.
He doesn`t quite know what to say before
this irrational barrage.

Nick smoothly steps in.

                    NICK
          Have you ever watched Mr.
          Spock on Star Trek?

Toomy looks at him, his voice getting even
louder.

                    TOOMY
          What in the hell are you
          talking about?!

                    NICK
          Just that if you don`t
          shut your gob at once,
          you bloody idiot, I`ll be
          happy to demonstrate his
          famous Vulcan sleeper-
          hold for you.

Toomy looks at him, his face suffusing
with blood. He snarls back.

                    TOOMY
          You can`t talk to me like
          that. Do you know who I
          am?

                    NICK
          Of course. You`re an
          obnoxious little bugger
          trying to hide his fear
          behind aggression. No
          harm in that, but you are
          in the way.

                    TOOMY
          You can`t talk to me like
          that. You`re not even an
          American citizen!

He takes a threatening step forward and
Nick moves in a blur.

His right hand snaps out and fastens on

to Toomy`s nose, holding it between his
first and second fingers. Toomy tries to
pull away, but Nick tightens his hold and
twists his hand slightly.

Toomy bellows in pain.

Nick`s voice suddenly drops a register to
a soft, dangerous whisper.

                    NICK
          I can break it. Easiest
          thing in the world,
          believe me.

Toomy begins to flail at him and Nick
twists his hand again.

Toomy bellows in pain once more.

                    NICK
          I don`t think you heard
          me. I can break it. Do
          you understand? Signify
          if you can understand?

He twists again. Toomy screams this time.
Just at that moment, Bethany Simms wanders
up.

She takes the situation in at a glance, an
appreciative smile flickering across her
face.

                    BETHANY
          Oh, wow, a nose-hold.

Nick and the others ignore her, Nick
leaning in and whispering to Toomy.

                    NICK
          I don`t have time to
          discuss your business
          appointments. Therefore,
          I am going to send you
          back to the cabin. This
          gentleman in the red
          shirt --

He glances at Don Gaffney who straightens
with a nod.

                  GAFFNEY
          Don Gaffney.

                    NICK
          Thank you.

Nick pulls Toomy closer, his voice getting
even more warm and confidential.

                    NICK
          Mr. Gaffney here will be
          your escort. Once you
          arrive in the main cabin,
          my buggardly friend, you
          will take a seat with
          your safety belt firmly
          fixed around your middle
          and keep your mouth shut.
          Do you understand?

Toomy manages to emit a pained, outraged
bellow.

                    NICK
          If you understand, please
          favor me with a thumbs
          up.

Toomy raises one thumb.

                    NICK
          Fine. I am going to let
          go of your nose now. When
          I do, if you so much as
          utter a single word,
          you will find yourself
          investigating hitherto
          unexplored realms of
          pain.

He lets go of Toomy`s nose and steps back.
Toomy stands there, staring at Nick with
angry, perplexed eyes. He raises a hand to
his nose and comes away with the tips of
his fingers bloody. He opens his mouth in
another bellow when Don Gaffney steps in.

                    GAFFNEY
          I wouldn`t, mister. Guy
          means it. You better come
          along with me.

He takes Toomy`s arm and gives it a gentle
tug. Toomy doesn`t move, his angry gaze
fixed on Nick. He opens his mouth again,
but Bethany chimes in, cutting him off.

                    BETHANY
          Bad idea.

Toomy closes his mouth and allows Gaffney to pull him back down the aisle toward the main cabin. Nick loses interest in him immediately and turns to Brian.

> NICK
> Ready to help me break
> down the door?

Brian nods and joins Nick in front of the door while Bethany watches, the two men positioning themselves to shoulder it open. Nick counts off.

> NICK
> Ready - one, two, _three_!

They dive toward the door.

INT. COCKPIT - NIGHT

The door pops open with absurd ease, Brian almost stumbling from his forward momentum, but Nick grabs him, steadying him. The two men straighten, looking about the cockpit. _It is empty, completely empty_.

The pilot`s controls move by themselves, the double wheels turning back and forth, left to right, making infinitesimal corrections necessary to keep the plane on its plotted course to Boston. The two small wings on the plane`s altitude indicator hold steady above an artificial horizon. Beyond the two small, slanted-forward windows, a billion stars twinkle in the darkness.

Bethany steps up behind the two men, peering over their shoulders to look at the silently moving flight sticks and the control board, lit up like a Christmas tree, different colored lights flicking on and off.

                    BETHANY
          Oh, wow. Nobody`s driving
          the plane.

ACT 2

INT. COCKPIT - NIGHT

Nick is the first to shake off his shock, nodding at a half empty cup of coffee and a partially eaten Danish on the service console beside the left arm of the co-pilot`s seat.

                    NICK
          It happened fast, whatever
          it was. Look there. And
          there.

He points first to the pilot`s seat, then to the floor beside the chair of the co-pilot.

Two wrist watches glimmer in the light of the controls, one a pressure-proof Rolex, the other a digital Pulsar.

Albert and Bob Jenkins join Bethany in the cockpit doorway, peering in at them.

                    ALBERT
          If you want watches, you
          can take your pick. There
          are tons of them back in
          the main cabin.

Brian and Nick look over their shoulders and see the two men behind Bethany.

                    NICK
          Are there indeed?

                  ALBERT
          Watches, jewelry, and
          glasses. Also purses. But
          the weirdest thing is -
          there`s stuff we`re pretty
          sure came from inside
          people. Like surgical
          pins and pacemakers.

Nick frowns and turns to Brian.

                    NICK
          I had been going on
          roughly the same
          assumption as our rude
          friend. The one I had
          to use the nose-lock
          on. That the plane set
          down someplace, for some
          reason, while I was
          asleep. That most of the
          passengers and the crew
          were somehow off loaded
          and then

Brian shakes his head.

                  BRIAN
          There couldn`t have been
          a take-off while we were
          sleeping. You can fly a
          plane on automatic, but
          you need a human being to
          take one up.

                    NICK
          So where did all the
          passengers and crew go?

                    BRIAN
          I don`t know, but I plan
          on finding out.

He slips into the pilot`s chair, checking
out the gauges on the control panel.

                    BRIAN
          Well, our altitude`s
          right, thirty six
          thousand feet, and we`re
          on course.

He reaches behind him and takes the
navigator`s chart book from a shelf, looks
at the airspeed indicator, and makes a
series of rapid calculations.

Nick, Albert, Bethany, and Bob watch.

                    NICK
          What are you doing?

                    BRIAN
          Figuring out our closest
          major airport.

Finished he sets aside the chart, puts on
the pilot`s headset, and flicks the toggle
switch turning on the radio.

He speaks into the headset.

> BRIAN
>
> Denver Central, this is
> American Pride Flight 29,
> over?

He flicks the toggle again and waits,
listening. Stunned amazement slips over
his face. Nick and the others can`t help
but see it.

> NICK
>
> What?

Brian ignores him, checking the transponder
setting. Then he flicks the toggle back to
transmit and tries again.

> BRIAN
>
> Denver Central, come in,
> please. This is American
> Pride Flight 29, and I
> have a problem. A big
> problem.

He listens some more. The worry in his
face deepens. It only makes the others
more anxious.

> NICK
>
> What is it?

> BRIAN
>
> I`m not getting anything.
> Anything at all.

He flicks back to the emergency band,
trying again as the others watch him in

slowly growing horror.

> **BRIAN**
> Mayday, Mayday, this is
> American Pride Flight 29
> requesting emergency aid.
> Come in, please.

He gets nothing, flicks to another band, and sends again.

> **BRIAN**
> UNICOM, this is American
> Pride Flight 29,
> requesting immediate
> radio contact. Over?

Still nothing.

He flicks back to the FAA emergency band, speaking into his headset, his voice rising with panic.

> **BRIAN**
> Denver, come in! Come in
> right now! <u>This is AP
> Flight 29, you answer me,
> goddammit</u>!

Nick reaches out, gently touching his shoulder.

> **NICK**
> Easy, mate.

Brian looks at him, his face flushed, his voice frantic.

                    BRIAN
          The dog won`t bark.
          Christ, what did they do,
          have a goddamn nuclear
          war?!

Nick looks at him, gripping his shoulder
more tightly.

                    NICK
          Easy. Tell me what you
          mean, the dog won`t bark.

                    BRIAN
          I mean Denver Control!
          That dog! I mean FAA
          Emergency. That dog!
          UNICOM, which gives
          advisories at small
          airports. That dog, too!
          I`ve never --

He suddenly reaches out, changing bands,
nodding at the control.

                    BRIAN
          Here, this is the medium-
          shortwave band. People
          should be jumping all
          over it like frogs on
          a hot side walk, but
          I can`t even pick up
          static.

He flicks another switch, looks up at
Albert, Bethany, and Bob who have crowded
in close.

                    BRIAN
          There`s no VOR beacon out
          of Denver either.

                     BOB
          Meaning?

                    BRIAN
          Meaning I have no
          radio. I have no Denver
          navigational beacon, and
          my board says everything
          is peachy keen. Which is
          crap. <u>Got</u> to be. According
          to my equipment, we`re
          less than fifty miles
          South of Denver right
          now.

He busies himself, rechecking the controls.
He throws a glance at Albert as he works.

                    BRIAN
          Hey, kid -- look out the
          window. Left side of the
          plane. Tell me what you
          see.

Albert steps to the small window on the
left side, peering out. He looks out for a
long time. Nick glances at him impatiently.

                     NICK
          Well?

Albert turns away from the window, looking
at them with horror struck eyes.

                    ALBERT
          There`s nothing out
          there. Nothing at all.

Brian takes off his head set, rises in his
seat, and peers out the window.

EXT. PLANE - NIGHT

There`s nothing down there in the darkness
below the plane except the dim outline of
long, sweeping, seemingly endless prairie.

INT. COCKPIT - NIGHT

Brian sits down, stunned, his legs suddenly
watery. Nick cuts him a glance, speaking
quietly.

                    NICK
          Denver`s blacked out,
          isn`t it?

Brian nods numbly, his face ghost white.

                    BRIAN
          Yes. Either that or gone.

He sinks into his seat, manically rechecking
his control board. Nick turns briskly to
Albert, Bob, and Bethany.

                    NICK
          All right, people! Back
          to your seats. I think we
          need a little quiet here.

Bethany looks at him questioningly, not wanting to leave.

                    BETHANY
          We are being quiet.

Bob turns to Albert and Bethany, putting an arm around each.

                     BOB
          Come, my young friends.
          Let`s go back and sit
          down. Our pilot has work
          to do.

The threesome leave, closing the cockpit door behind them as Nick turns back to Brian who sits hunched over the control board, his fingers flying.

                     NICK
          What are you doing?

                    BRIAN
          Using the military-
          aircraft band. Strategic
          Air Command in Omaha is
          never off the air, no
          matter what.
               (into the headset mike)
          Air Force Control, this
          is American Pride Flight
          29. Do you read me? Over.

INT. COACH SECTION - NIGHT

Albert, Bethany, and Bob walk into Coach

Class to find Laurel seated with Dinah, still holding her hand, and behind them, farther back, Don Gaffney and Craig Toomy. They sit to either end of the aisle, studiously ignoring each other. Bob and his small group come to a halt around Laurel and Dinah. Albert and Bethany slide into seats while Bob remains standing. Gaffney looks up at him.

                    GAFFNEY
          What`s going on?

                    BOB
          The pilot and the British
          fellow are trying to
          raise an airport on the
          radio.
                    (a beat, then)
          I suppose we should all
          get to know each other.
          My name is Bob Jenkins
          and I`m a mystery writer.
          Written over forty novels
          and none of them as
          strange as this.

Finished, he looks at the others, waiting. Laurel is the first to speak.

                    LAUREL
          I`m Laurel Stevenson. I`m
          a school teacher in the
          San Fernando Valley and
          this is --

Laurel hesitates, then continues.

                    LAUREL
          -- the first vacation
          I`ve had in eight years.

Dinah turns, looking at her.

Her brows knit as though what Laurel
has said -- or the way she`s said it is
bothering her.

Laurel notices.

                    LAUREL
          Is something wrong,
          Dinah?

A beat, then Dinah shakes her head, staring
at the others.

                    DINAH
          My name is Dinah Bellman
          and I`m on my way to
          have an eye operation in
          Boston. Afterwards, I`ll
          be able to see again.
          <u>Probably</u> be able to
          see again. The doctors
          say there`s a seventy
          percent chance I`ll get
          some vision and a forty
          percent chance I`ll get
          all of it.

Albert looks around.

It seems to be his turn.

                    ALBERT
          Albert Kaussner. I`m on
          my way to the Berkeley
          School of Music outside
          Boston.

He stands up, opening an overhead rack and
pulling out a violin case. He shows it to
the others.

                    ALBERT
          I play violin.

He sits, hugging the instrument to his
chest. Bethany is next.

                    BETHANY
          I`m Bethany Simms. I was
          going to spend a few
          days with my Aunt in
          Worcester, Mass., but now
          --

She drifts into silence.

Bob nods and looks toward the back of
the plane where Craig Toomy sits, staring
off into space, plucking the edges of a
magazine.

                    BOB
          What about you, sir?
          What`s your name?

Toomy`s gaze slowly rises to Bob Jenkins.
He stares at the elderly writer with dead
eyes, not saying anything.

Bob sees he is not going to get a response and shifts his gaze to Don Gaffney.

                    BOB
          What about you, Mr.
          Gaffney? What do you do?

                  GAFFNEY
          Tool and dye worker for
          Hughes Aircraft. On my
          way to visit my first
          grandchild in Boston.

Bob nods, satisfied.

                    BOB
          Well, now we all know
          each other. That leaves
          us with the Sixty-four
          Thousand Dollar Question.
          What the hell is going
          on?

They all stare back at him silently.

Obviously no one feels they have the right answer or even one remotely close.

INT. COCKPIT - NIGHT

Brian suddenly gives up on calling for help, and snaps the radio off.

He turns stricken eyes on Nick, eyes that say he`s coming unglued, that this is finally all too much for him.

                    BRIAN
          That dog won`t bark
          either. None of them
          will. We`re all alone up
          here. <u>Completely, totally</u>
          <u>all alone</u>!

Nick clamps a hand on him, high up on his
shoulder, near his neck. He leans in so
close their noses almost touch.

                    NICK
          Now listen to me, my
          friend, and listen well:
          <u>panic is not allowed</u>.
          There are a dozen people
          on this plane, and your
          job is the same as it
          ever was: to bring them
          down in one piece.

Brian looks at him, a little testy as the
panic recedes.

                    BRIAN
          You don`t need to tell me
          what my job is.

Nick smiles, claps him on the back, and
sits back.

                    NICK
          I`m afraid I did, but
          you`re looking a hundred
          percent better now.

Brian looks at him, still a bit shaky, his

eyes filling with curiosity.

                    BRIAN
          What do you do for
          a living, Nick? And
          don`t tell me you`re an
          accountant.

Nick throws back his head and laughs. It`s
a welcome sound in this cockpit.

                    NICK
          Junior attaché, British
          embassy, old man.

                    BRIAN
          My aunt`s hat.

Nick shrugs, smiling softly now.

                    NICK
          Well -- that`s what it
          says on my papers. If
          they said anything else,
          I suppose it would be Her
          Majesty`s Mechanic. I fix
          things that need fixing.
          Right now that means you.

                    BRIAN
          Thank you, but I`m fixed.

                    NICK
          All right, then -- what do
          you mean to do? Can you
          navigate without those
          ground-beam thingies? Can

                    NICK (CONT.)
you avoid other planes?

                    BRIAN
I can navigate just
fine with the on board
equipment. As for other
planes --

He points to the green radar screen with
its constantly circling sweeper. There`s
not a blip on it.

                    BRIAN
This bastard says there
<u>aren`t</u> any other planes.

                    NICK
Well, at least we don`t
have to worry about
running into anybody
then. Do you intend to
continue on to Boston?

                    BRIAN
Logan at dawn, with no
idea what`s going on in
the country below us? No
way. We`re heading for
Bangor, Maine and I think
it`s time to tell the
passengers. The few that
are left anyway.

He picks up the microphone, about to
broadcast over the jet PA system when the
bald man who had been sleeping so soundly

in the business section with Nick, sticks his head into the cockpit, looking at them with a yawn. He is in his 50s, wears a brown business suit, and his name is RUDY WARWICK.

> RUDY
> Would one of you gentleman
> be so kind as to tell me
> what`s happened to all
> the service personnel?
> I`ve had a very nice nap
> -- but now I`d like my
> dinner.

Brian and Nick can only stare at him, so surprised to see him that both are momentarily stumped for an answer.

Nick is the first to get his tongue unstuck.

> NICK
> I`m afraid we have a
> small problem --

INT. COACH CLASS - NIGHT

The small group in coach, excluding Craig Toomy who stares at nothing and Don Gaffney who keeps a wary eye on him, continue their discussion about their situation.

> ALBERT
> (caught mid-sentence)
> -- but it doesn`t make
> any sense. Where`d
> everybody go?

                    BOB
          I don`t know, but perhaps
          --

The PA system suddenly snaps to life.

                    BRIAN (V.O.)
          Ladies and gentlemen,
          this is the Captain
          speaking.

Craig Toomy jerks upright. His lips pull
back over his teeth in a nasty snarl.

                    TOOMY
          Captain, my ass!

Gaffney sits erect, staring at him from
across the aisle.

                    GAFFNEY
          Shut up!

Toomy looks at him, startled, and subsides
as Brian continues over the address system.

                    BRIAN (V.O.)
          As you know, we have an
          extremely odd situation
          on our hands here. I
          have no cockpit-to-
          ground communication.
          And about five minutes
          ago we should have been
          able to see the lights of
          Denver clearly from the
          airplane. We couldn`t.

Laurel reaches out and takes Dinah`s hand and grips it firmly.

Albert lets out a low, awed whistle and sinks down further in his chair. Bethany sits frozen in hers, her eyes squeezed tightly shut. Bob Jenkins stares off into space, listening to every word, his hands resting on his lap.

> BRIAN (V.O.) (CONT.)
> All of that is bad news.
> The good news is this:
> the plane is undamaged,
> we have plenty of fuel,
> and I`m qualified to fly
> this make and model. The
> last thing I want to pass
> on to you is that our
> destination will now be
> Bangor, Maine.

Craig Toomy sits up with a bellow.

> TOOMY

Whaaat!?

> BRIAN (V.O.)
> Our in-flight navigation
> equipment is in five-by-
> five working order, but
> I can`t say the same for
> our navigational beams.
> Under these circumstances,
> Bangor International
> Airport is our safest bet
> --

Toomy bawls again, this time in an even louder voice.

                    TOOMY
          I have an important
          business meeting at the
          Pru this morning at nine
          o`clock AND I FORBID YOU
          TO FLY INTO SOME WHISTLE
          STOP MAINE AIRPORT!

He unlatches his seat belt and stands. His cheeks are red, his brow waxy, and his eyes frighteningly blank. He bellows again.

                    TOOMY
          DO YOU UNDERSTAND --

Laurel feels Dinah`s chest hitch and she realizes the little girl is about burst into tears. She twists in her seat, looking back at Toomy.

                    LAUREL
          Please, mister, keep
          your voice down. You`re
          scaring the little girl.

Toomy turns that frightening blank gaze on her and Dinah.

                    TOOMY
SCARING THE LITTLE GIRL? WE`RE DIVERTING
TO SOME TIN POT AIRPORT IN THE MIDDLE OF
NOWHERE, AND

                    TOOMY (CONT.)
            ALL YOU`VE GOT TO WORRY
            ABOUT IS --

Don Gaffney suddenly stands, staring at
Toomy.

                    GAFFNEY
            Sit down and shut up or
            I`ll pop you one.

Toomy`s upper lip pulls back in a snarl of
contempt.

                    TOOMY
            I don`t think you could
            do it alone, pops.

Rudy Warwick, the bald man from Business
Class, suddenly steps into their cabin,
staring at Toomy.

                    RUDY
            He won`t have to. I`ll
            take a swing at you
            myself if you don`t shut
            up.

Toomy stares at him, about to reply when
Albert suddenly stands, staring at him,
working hard to muster his courage.

                    ALBERT
            I`ll help them if you
            don`t shut up, mister. I
            really will.

                        65

Toomy stares at him, hatred flooding his eyes and right behind it, flickering, incipient insanity. Dinah senses it, and stiffens in her seat. Behind her, Toomy continues to stare at Albert.

FLASHCUT - TOOMY`S POV OF ALBERT - NIGHT

Albert`s face suddenly seems to shimmer and slide, the features rearranging themselves into a gargoyle aspect, still Albert`s face, but now horribly transformed into that of a gibbering, blood-thirsty monster.

INT. COACH CABIN - NIGHT

Dinah jerks upright in her seat, tensing even more as she establishes psychic contact and slips inside Toomy`s head.

FLASHCUT - INSIDE DINAH`S HEAD - NIGHT

Toomy`s POV of Albert -- even more distorted and monstrous.

INT. CABIN - NIGHT (BACK INTO REALITY)

Toomy tears his gaze from Albert and swings it to Rudy Warwick. In the forward seat, Dinah`s head moves in the same direction.

FLASHCUT - INSIDE DINAH`S HEAD - NIGHT

Toomy`s POV of Rudy Warwick -- even more

distorted and monstrous than his previous vision of Albert, warts and sores covering his face, pus running down his cheeks, his nose huge and long, shaggy hair covering his forehead.

INT. COACH CABIN - NIGHT (BACK INTO REALITY)

Toomy swings his gaze to Don Gaffney. Dinah twitches, her body rigid, still seeing through Toomy's eyes as her head moves in the same direction.

FLASHCUT -INSIDE DINAH'S HEAD - NIGHT

Toomy's POV of Don Gaffney. The tool and dye worker looks even worse than Rudy Warwick, like some kind of evil troll inside a middle-aged man's body, staring back at Toomy with an awful, gobbling hunger. Toomy's gaze moves on to Don Gaffney and Laurel, both of whom also look like monsters, finally stopping on Dinah.

INT. CABIN - NIGHT (BACK INTO REALITY) 4

Dinah sits breathless in her seat, Toomy staring at her, she staring through Toomy's eyes at herself.

FLASHCUT - TOOMY'S POV OF HERSELF
THROUGH TOOMY'S EYES

She suddenly transmogrifies, turning into the most monstrous of them all -- a piggish teenager with a baby face and eyes hidden behind huge black lenses, two enormous fangs poking out of the side of her mouth, slobber dripping down her suddenly hairy chin.

INT. COACH CABIN - NIGHT (BACK INTO REALITY)

Toomy shakes his head, snapping out of his psychotic episode.

In the forward seat, Dinah shakes her head, the psychic contact with Toomy broken. He stares at the others.

His lips curl into a sneer.

> TOOMY
> I see. You`re all against
> me.

He abruptly sits, picks up a cocktail napkin lying on the arm of the seat next to him and begins plucking at it. Don Gaffney stares at him.

> GAFFNEY
> Doesn`t have to be this
> way, mister. You ought to
> just relax and take it
> easy.

Toomy cuts a brief glance in Gaffney`s direction, then looks back at the cocktail napkin.

He slowly, carefully begins to tear it
into long strips. Rudy breaks in.

                    RUDY
          Anyone here know how to
          run that little oven in
          the galley?

The others stare back at him. No one
answers.

He shrugs sadly.

                    RUDY
          I didn`t think so. This is
          the era of specialization.
          A shameful time to be
          alive.

He turns and disappears back into business
section. The others start to relax a bit.
Laurel turns, looking at Dinah. Beneath
the rims of her dark glasses, the girl`s
cheeks are wet with tears. Laurel forgets
her own fears and gives her a hug.

                    LAUREL
          Don`t cry, honey -- that
          man was just upset. He`s
          better now.

Dinah wipes away her tears and leans in,
whispering to her.

                    DINAH
          We all look like monsters
          to him.

                    LAUREL
          Oh, no, I`m sure we
          don`t. What would make
          you think a thing like
          that?

Dinah replies hesitantly, but excitedly.

                    DINAH
          I - I hear things
          sometimes. People`s
          thoughts. Always have.
          But just now, for the
          first time -- I saw what
          that man was seeing --
          it was dark and fuzzy,
          but I still saw.

                    LAUREL
          Oh, Dinah, that`s just
          your imagination, that`s
          all.

                    DINAH
          That`s what my aunt used
          to say too. But it`s not.

Laurel looks at her, sees she is dead
serious, and tries to humor her.

                    LAUREL
          Why don`t you try getting
          some sleep, honey.
          That`ll make you feel
          better.

Dinah sighs, a watery, unhappy sound.

                    DINAH
          No, it won't. Besides, I
          was asleep and now I'm
          all slept out.

In the seat two rows back, Bob lifts his
head, listening to the girl's words. His
brows knit in thought. Her words have
reminded him of something.   Something
important, if he could only remember what.

EXT. 767 - A LITTLE LATER THAT NIGHT

The plane cruises through the night, the
only sound the soft drone of its jets.

INT. COACH CLASS - NIGHT

Albert stares out the window, lost in
thought. Bob Jenkins suddenly plops into
the seat next to him, looking at him
intently.

                    BOB
          Do you remember what that
          little girl said earlier?

Albert looks at Bob, slightly confused.

                    ALBERT
          Unh -no, not really.

                    BOB
          She told Miss Stevenson
          she didn't think she
          could get back to sleep

                    BOB (CONT.)
because she had been
sleeping. I was also
sleeping. What about you,
dear boy?

                    ALBERT
What about me what?

                    BOB
Were you asleep? You
were, weren`t you?

                    ALBERT
Well, yeah.

                    BOB
We were <u>all</u> asleep. The
people who disappeared
were all awake --

Albert spends a moment thinking about
this, then:

                    ALBERT
Well -- maybe.

                    BOB
Nonsense. I write
mysteries for a living.
Deduction is my bread
and butter. Don`t you
think if someone had
been awake when all those
people were eliminated,
that person would have
screamed bloody murder,

BOB (CONT.)
waking the rest of us?

ALBERT
I guess so.

BOB
Correct. So I deduce that
only waking passengers
were subtracted. Along
with the flight crew, of
course, dear boy.

ALBERT
Could you call me Albert,
Mr. Jenkins, please?
That`s my name.

Bob is immediately apologetic, patting
Albert on the shoulder.

BOB
I`m sorry. I`m upset,
and when I`m upset, I
have a tendency to be
patronizing. Please,
forgive me. It`s just
that I`m trying to figure
out what happened.

ALBERT
Do you have any ideas?

BOB
Well, if it were just the
plane, I suppose I could
come up with a scenario.

                    ALBERT
What scenario?

                     BOB
Well, for instance, let
us say some shadowy
government organization
decided to carry out
an experiment, and we
are the test subjects.
The purpose of such an
experiment, given the
circumstances, might be
to document the affects
of severe emotional
distress on a number
of average Americans.
The scientists running
the experiment load
the airplane`s oxygen
system with some sort of
odorless hypnotic drug.
After it is released into
the air, everyone falls
asleep, except for the
pilot who is breathing
uncontaminated air
through a mask.

                    ALBERT
But --

Jenkins smiles and raises a hand.

                     BOB
I know what your objection
is, Albert, and I can

                    BOB (CONT.)
          explain it. Allow me?

Albert nods. Jenkins continues.

                         BOB
          The pilot lands the plane
          at a secret airstrip --
          in Nevada, let us say.
          The passengers and flight
          crew who were awake when
          the gas was released are
          off-loaded. The passengers
          who were asleep -- you
          and I among them --
          simply go on sleeping.
          The pilot then returns
          flight 29 to its proper
          altitude and heading. He
          engages the auto pilot.
          As the plane reaches the
          Rockies, the affects of
          the gas begin to wear
          off. Over his intercom,
          the pilot can hear the
          little blind girl crying
          out for her aunt. He
          knows she will wake the
          others. The experiment
          is about to begin. So he
          gets up and leaves the
          cockpit, taking a seat
          among the slowly waking
          passengers.

Albert listens, his face congealing with
horror.

                    ALBERT
          Captain Engle is one of
          them?

Jenkins nods.

                    JENKINS
          In my scenario.

Neither of them notice Craig Toomy sit up
behind them two rows back where he has
been resting.

He has heard every word and stares at
them over the seat tops with glittering,
feverish eyes. Albert, totally unaware
of Toomy, sits there stunned by Bob`s
revelation.

                    ALBERT
          If Captain Engle is one
          of the people who did
          this to us, we`ll have to
          capture him as soon as we
          land.

                    BOB
          But it doesn`t stand up,
          you know.

Albert stares at him, stunned by this
latest revelation.

                    ALBERT
          What? What doesn`t stand
          up?

                    BOB
          The scenario I just
          outlined for you.

                  ALBERT
          But you just said

                    BOB
          I said <u>if it were just
          the plane</u>, I could come
          up with a scenario.
          Unfortunately, it <u>isn`t</u>
          just the plane. Denver
          might still have been
          down there, but all the
          lights were off if it was
          and I can tell you it`s
          not just Denver either.
          I have been coordinating
          our route of travel with
          my wristwatch. Omaha,
          Des Moines, St. Louis
          -- no sign of them down
          there in the dark either,
          Albert. No, whatever is
          happening is not just
          going on inside the
          plane. And that is where
          deduction breaks down.

Albert stares at him, more confused than
ever.

                  ALBERT
          Than what is happening?

Jenkins utters a long, uneasy sigh.

> JENKINS
> I`m the wrong person to
> ask. Too bad Larry Niven
> or John Varley isn`t on
> board.

> ALBERT
> Who are those guys?

> JENKINS
> Science fiction writers.

Two rows back Craig Toomy slips out of his seat and down the aisle to a seat further toward the back. There he sits, pondering the words he has heard, his face twisting with barely suppressed rage as he mutters to himself.

> TOOMY
> I`m not going to be
> anybody`s guinea pig. Not
> the government`s, not my
> company`s, and especially
> not Captain Engle`s.

With that he tears a long strip of paper loose from a magazine cover he holds, RIPPP, and lets it float to the floor at his feet.

ACT 3

INT. COCKPIT - NIGHT

Nick watches as Brian continues to call on the radio.

> BRIAN
> St. Louis Central, come
> in, please. This is
> American Pride Flight 29,
> repeat, American Pride
> Flight 29, over.

Nothing. He toggles the radio off and tosses his head mic, shaking his head in frustration.

> BRIAN
> Nothing anywhere. Not
> on the ground or in the
> air. It`s like the entire
> country has suddenly
> ceased to exist.

> NICK
> I don`t suppose you read
> science fiction, do you?

> BRIAN
> I was crazy about it as a
> kid, you?

Nick smiles.

                    NICK
          Until I was eighteen or
          so. I`ve been sitting here
          and running all those
          old stories through my
          head, matey. And thinking
          about such exotic things
          as time-warps and space-
          warps and alien raiding
          parties. I mean, we don`t
          really have any way of
          knowing if <u>anything</u> is
          left down there, do we?
          Especially not with this
          cloud cover.

He half-rises, staring out the window.

EXT. PLANE - NIGHT

Below, and to every side of them, cloud
cover blots out the earth below.

It`s like they`re flying with nothing
below them, but a feathery, white pillow.

INT. COCKPIT - NIGHT

Brian looks up at Nick as he flies the
plane.

                    BRIAN
          No, we don`t. And it
          might hold all the way
          to Bangor. With Air
          Traffic Control out of
          commission, there`s no

                    BRIAN (CONT.)
way of knowing.

Nick sinks back in his seat, looking at
him.

                    NICK
          Suppose you took us down?
          Just for a quick look-
          see.

Brian considers this for a moment, then
shakes his head.

                    BRIAN
          Too dangerous with no ATC
          and no other planes to
          talk to. You can laugh at
          me if you want --

                    NICK
          I`m not laughing, matey.
          I`m not even close to
          laughing. Believe me.

                    BRIAN
          Well, suppose we have
          slipped into another
          dimension, like in a
          science story. How do we
          know what`s down there?
          This earth could have the
          Rockies in upstate New
          York, or we could run
          into a rocket shuttle, or
          God knows what.

Nick nods out the window.

                    NICK
          We seem to have the sky
          pretty much to ourselves.

                    BRIAN
          Up here, that`s true.
          Down there, who knows?
          And "who knows" is a very
          dicey situation for an
          airline pilot. I intend
          to overfly Bangor when
          we get there, if these
          clouds still hold. I`ll
          take us over the Atlantic
          and drop under the
          ceiling as we head back.
          Our odds will be better
          if we make our initial
          descent over water.

                    NICK
          So for now, we just go
          on?

                    BRIAN
          Right.

                    NICK
          And wait.

                    BRIAN
          Right again.

Nick sighs.

                    NICK
          Well, you`re the captain.

Brian smiles.

                    BRIAN
          That`s three in a row.

EXT. SKY - DAWN

Dawn comes up as Flight 29 drones through
the air, a few hundred feet above the
solid carpet of cloud cover that obscures
the ground and seems endless, stretching
for miles in every direction.

INT. CABIN SECTION - DAY

Toward the front of the cabin section,
Dinah awakens, stretching and yawning.
Laurel, seated next to her, throws her a
smile she cannot see.

                    LAUREL
          Feeling better?

                    DINAH
          A little.
               (a beat, then)
          I don`t mean to pry, but

                    LAUREL
          Go on, ask anything you
          want.

> DINAH
> Why did you lie about why
> you were going to Boston?

Laurel stares at the girl, startled.

> LAUREL
> How did you know I lied?

> DINAH
> I could hear it in your
> voice. I can hear lots
> of things. Maybe because
> I`m blind, I don`t know.
> But I know you don`t lie.
> Otherwise I wouldn`t have
> heard the difference.

Laurel smiles and lays her head back on
the pillow.

> LAUREL
> I`m going to -- no, I was
> going to meet someone. A
> man named Darren Crosby.

> DINAH
> How did you come to know
> him?

> LAUREL
> Well, that`s the
> embarrassing part. And
> why I lied. I never have
> actually met him. We
> started corresponding
> through the personal ads

                    LAUREL (CONT.)
in a magazine and I liked
him. Liked what he wrote
anyway and how he looked
in his picture. So I
agreed to fly to Boston
to meet him.

                    DINAH
That`s strange, isn`t
it? To fly all the way
across the country to see
someone you`ve never even
met before.

Laurel can`t help smiling.

                    LAUREL
Yes, but I just realized
it really didn`t have
anything to do with
Mister Crosby. It had to
do with me. I didn`t want
to play it safe anymore.
I was trying to break
out of the safe confines
of my life and have an
adventure.

She breaks into a laugh, looking around
her.

                    LAUREL
I`m afraid I got more
adventure than I ever
bargained for.

Dinah reaches out, touching Laurel`s face.

She slowly runs her hand across her features, her nose, her mouth, her eyes.

The blind girl smiles.

>   DINAH
> You`re very pretty,
> Laurel. I`m sure you`ll
> find what you`re looking
> for.

With that she nestles her head on Laurel`s breast and closes her eyes, dozing off again.

A moment later Bethany Simms drops into the window seat across the aisle from Laurel.

Laurel watches as she looks out the window.

>   LAUREL
> What do you see?

>   BETHANY
> Well, the sun`s up, but
> that`s all.

>   LAUREL
> What about the ground?

Bethany stares out. All she sees is that carpet of clouds below them.

>   BETHANY
> Can`t see it. It`s all

                    BETHANY (CONT.)
clouds down there.

                    LAUREL
Maybe it`s better that
way.

                    BETHANY
Maybe. Do you think we`ll
be all right?

                    LAUREL
I think so. I hope so.

                    BETHANY
I`m scared about what
might be under those
clouds, but I was scared
anyway. About Boston.
My mother all at once
decided how it would be a
great idea if I spent a
couple of weeks with my
Aunt Shawna. I think the
idea was for me to get
off the plane, and then
Shawna pulls the string
on me.

                    LAUREL
What string?

                    BETHANY
Do not pass Go, do not
collect two hundred
dollars, go directly to
the nearest rehab center,

>   BETHANY (CONT.)
>   and stay there until
>   you`ve dried out.

She stops for a breath, runs her hands
through her short dark hair.

>   BETHANY
>   Things were already so
>   weird that this seems
>   like just more of the
>   same.
>   (a beat, then)
>   This is really happening,
>   isn`t it? I mean I`m not
>   just imagining it, am I?

>   LAUREL
>   No. It`s real enough, I`m
>   afraid.
>   (a beat, then)
>   Do you need a rehab,
>   Bethany?

>   BETHANY
>   I don`t know.

She turns, looks out the window at the
carpet of clouds below.

Her smile fades and her voice turns morose.

>   BETHANY
>   I guess I might. I used
>   to think it was just
>   party time, but now I

                    BETHANY (CONT.)
          don`t know. But getting
          shipped off this way --
          I feel like a pig in a
          slaughterhouse chute.

                    LAUREL
          I`m sorry.

                    BETHANY
          I`m sorry, too, but I
          guess this is the wrong
          time to worry about it,
          huh?
                    (a beat, then)
          You don`t have any grass,
          do you?

                    LAUREL
          I`m afraid not.

                    BETHANY
          Well, you`re one ahead
          of me -- I`m just plain
          afraid.

EXT. SKY - DAY

The 727 cruises through a full morning sun
shining from above, the endless cloud bank
below.

INT. COCKPIT - DAY

Nick watches as Brian finishes checking
his heading, air speed, navigational
figures, and finally his chart. Last of

all he checks his wrist watch. Two minutes
past eight.

                    BRIAN
          Well, I think it`s about
          time to fish or cut bait.

He reaches forward and flashes on the
FASTEN SEAT BELT sign. The bell makes its
low, pleasant chime. Then he flicks the
intercom toggle and picks up the mike.

                    BRIAN
          Hello, ladies and
          gentlemen. This is
          Captain Engle again.
          We`re currently over the
          Atlantic Ocean, roughly
          thirty miles east of the
          Maine coast. I`ll be
          commencing our initial
          descent into the Bangor
          area very soon.

INT. MAIN CABIN - DAY

All the passengers rouse themselves,
buckling their safety belts as they listen
tensely to Brian`s words over the intercom.

                    BRIAN (V.O.)
          I want you to make sure
          your seat belts are snug
          and secure.

Laurel snugs down Dinah`s seat belt
tightly.

Bob and Albert exchange tense glances.

Further forward, Bethany bends her head in a silent prayer. Toomy just stares vacantly ahead, continuing to tear paper into strips. Don Gaffney sits across the aisle, trying to ignore the irritating habit as he listens to Brian.

                    BRIAN (V.O.)
          I`m beginning our descent
          now. Please be calm; my
          board is green across and
          all procedures here on
          the flight deck remain
          routine.

INT. COCKPIT - DAY

Finished, Brian hangs the microphone up and brings the plane around in a long slow turn. Nick watches him.

                    NICK
          Very comforting that.
          You should have been a
          politician, matey.

The seats beneath him and Brian cant slightly forward as the 767 begins its slow descent toward the clouds at 4,000 feet.

                    BRIAN
          I doubt they`re feeling
          very comfortable right
          now. I know I`m not.

                    (checking his instrument board)
                30,000 feet and still
                descending.

EXT. SKY - DAY

The 767 takes a long dive out of the wan
sun toward the clouds below.

INT. COCKPIT - DAY

Nick stares out the window at the white
featureless clouds that seem to be rushing
up at them.

They stretch from horizon to horizon like
some strange ballroom floor. Nick breaks
the silence in a suddenly hoarse voice.

                    NICK
            I don`t mind telling you
            I`m afraid, matey. Part
            of me would like to grab
            you and make you take us
            right back up.

                    BRIAN
            It wouldn`t do any good.
            We can`t stay up here
            forever.

                    NICK
            I know, but I`m still
            afraid of what`s under
            those clouds. Or not
            under them.

                    BRIAN
          Well, we`ll find out
          together.

EXT. SKY - DAY

The 767 keeps diving, passing through
25,000 feet, still descending.

INT. MAIN CABIN - DAY

Rudy Warwick, the bald-headed businessman,
enters from business class and grabs a
seat in the middle section. He looks at
the passengers closest to him, Laurel and
Dinah.

                    RUDY
          Figure we might as well
          all be together on this
          one.

He straps himself in as the plane continues
to descend, the cabin canting farther
forward as the angle steepens. The only
sounds are the soft drone of the jets and
the <u>rii-ip rii-ip rii-ip</u> of Craig Toomy
dismembering another in-flight magazine.
Don Gaffney finally can`t stand it anymore
and cuts him an irritated glance.

                    GAFFNEY
          Would you mind stopping
          that? It`s driving me
          crazy!

Toomy turns and regards Don Gaffney with

a pair of wide, smooth, empty eyes. Turns his head back. Holds up the page he is currently working on and slowly tears it. <u>Rii-ip</u>. Gaffney opens his mouth to say something, then closes it tight. Laurel slips her arm around Dinah`s shoulder. Dinah takes her hand and squeezes it. Bethany sits alone, staring out a window, her body held so stiffly upright it might be wired together. The plane shudders slightly as it continues its descent. Rudy raises his head and yells to the rest

                    RUDY
          Well, at least we`ll be
          able to get some chow
          when we land.

No one answers. The main cabin is encased in a stiff shell of tension. Albert gnaws on his lower lip and leans over, staring out the window at the clouds rushing up at him from below.

EXT. PLANE - DAY

The plane continues its descent toward the clouds. They have lost their flat look; fluffy curves and mild crenulations filled with early morning shadows can be seen. The plane continues its descent, slipping beneath 18,000 feet.

INT. MAIN CABIN - DAY

Laurel pulls back from the window. She talks to Dinah, happy to hear the sound of any voice, even her own.

                    LAUREL
          You know something,
          Dinah?

Dinah looks in her direction.

                    DINAH
          What?

                    LAUREL
          I really don`t want to
          go down there. I mean, I
          <u>really</u> don`t.

                    DINAH
          Well, if it will make you
          feel any better, you`re
          not the only one.

The woman and the young girl grip each
other tighter. Bethany suddenly speaks up
in a thin, watery voice.

                    BETHANY
          I`m scared. I mean very
          scared.

She unbuckles and moves away from the
window seat to one in the center section,
fastens the lap-belt, and presses her
hands tightly against her middle, rocking
forward slightly.

                    BETHANY
          I think I`m going to pass

                    BETHANY (CONT.)
          out.

Behind her, Craig Toomy cuts her a glance
and rips a fresh strip of paper from a
route map. Albert sits in his seat across
the aisle, several rows back, staring at
the girl. After a moment, he unbuckles
himself, gets up, and sits down beside
Bethany, and buckles up again. She
immediately grasps his hands. He speaks,
trying to sound brave, but what comes out
is the voice of a scared seventeen-year
old violin student who feels on the verge
of passing out himself.

                    ALBERT
          It`s going to be all
          right.

                    BETHANY
          I hope --

The plane suddenly bucks up and down,
lifting the passengers an inch or more
out of their seats. Bethany screams at the
top of her lungs. Dinah looks up, blindly
searching for the source of the scream.
Her own voice fills with dread.

                    DINAH
          What`s wrong? Is something
          wrong with the plane? Are
          we going to crash?

Laurel grabs her even harder, holding on
for dear life.

                    LAUREL
          I don`t think so, honey.
          I hope not anyway.

Brian`s voice suddenly comes over the
intercom. It sounds as though he is making
a supreme effort to keep calm and failing.

                    BRIAN (V.O.)
          This is ordinary light
          turbulence, folks. Most
          of you have been through
          this before so just
          settle down.

The intercom goes dead as he clicks off.
Rii-ip goes another strip of paper as Toomy
shreds it. Gaffney cuts him a killing look.
Bob leans over, staring out the window.

EXT. SKY - DAY

The plane continues its descent, its shadow
rippling across the white surface of the
clouds just below.

INT. MAIN CABIN - DAY

Bob leans back, grabbing his armrests with
either hand and holding on for dear life.
He mutters to himself.

                    BOB
          God help us all. Please.

Farther down the aisle, Dinah squeezes

Laurel`s hand even more tightly.

> DINAH
> Is it going to be all
> right? Is it really going
> to be all right?

Laurel looks out the window. Wisps of cotton-candy clouds are whipping by outside.

EXT. SKY - DAY

The 767 skims the tops of the clouds.

INT. MAIN CABIN - DAY

The plane hits a series of jolts and Laurel has to close her throat against a moan. She renews her grip on Dinah.

> LAUREL
> I hope so, honey. I hope
> so.

INT. COCKPIT - DAY

Brian sits at the stick, piloting the plane along the top of the cloud bank. Chunks of clouds whip by outside the window. Nick watches them obscure his view with growing disquiet.

> NICK
> Maybe this isn`t such a
> good idea. Maybe we`d

                    NICK (CONT.)
          better climb back up and
          think this over --

Brian`s eyes are locked to the
instrumentation as he replies.

                    BRIAN
          Not enough time and not
          enough fuel.

The plane begins to bounce again, harder
this time. Brian makes corrections
automatically.

                    BRIAN
          Hang on. We`re going in.

He pushes the wheel forward even more. The
altimeter needle begins to move swiftly
beneath its glass circle.

EXT. SKY - DAY

Flight 29 slides into the cloud bank. For
a moment it`s tail protrudes, cutting
through the fluffy surface like the fin
of a shark. A moment later the 767 slides
into the cloud bank and disappears.

ACT 4

INT. MAIN CABIN - DAY

Inside the cabin it goes from bright sunlight to the gloom of late twilight. The plane begins to buck harder. There is one particularly hard bump and with a startled sigh, Bethany faints. Albert grabs her, forgetting his own panic. He shakes her.

                    ALBERT
          Bethany? Bethany?!

No response as the plane leaps again.

INT. FIRST-CLASS CABIN - DAY

The drinks trolley suddenly rolls to the right across the aisle and slams into the bulkhead. Tiny little liquor bottles and empty glasses rattle on the metal trolley, several of them crashing to the floor.

INT. MAIN CABIN - DAY

Dinah shrieks at the sound. Gaffney lets out a terrified yell as he holds on to his armrests with white knuckles.

                    GAFFNEY
          For God`s sakes, what was
          that?!

Bob yells back in a hoarse voice.

>   BOB
>   The drink trolley. It was
>   left out, remember? I
>   think it must have rolled
>   across --

The plane goes into another dizzying
roller coaster leap and comes down with a
jarring smack.

INT. FIRST-CLASS CABIN - DAY

The drinks trolley takes off down the aisle
toward the front of the plane, gathering
speed as it smashes into the bulkhead
separating First from Business Class and
overturns with a glass splintering crash.

INT. MAIN CABIN - DAY

Dinah shrieks again and wraps her arms
around Laurel, almost squeezing her to
death.

Laurel struggles, trying to loosen the
girl`s grip.

>   LAUREL
>   It`s all right. Don`t
>   hold me so tight, Dinah,
>   honey --

Dinah shrieks at the top of her lungs.

> DINAH
> Please, I don`t want to
> die! I just don`t want to
> die!

Brian`s voice suddenly comes over the intercom.

> BRIAN (V.O.)
> A little unexpected
> turbulence, folks. Just
> be calm --

Another rocketing, twisting bump. Another crash from Business Section as more glasses and mini-bottles fall out of the overturned drinks trolley. From across the aisle on Don Gaffney`s left Toomy tears another strip of paper. <u>Rii-ip</u>! Gaffney turns to Toomy, his face scarlet with fear, but his eyes flashing with fury.

> GAFFNEY
> Quit it right now,
> asshole, or I`ll stuff
> what`s left of that
> magazine right down your
> throat.

Toomy looks at him blandly, seemingly oblivious to their wild descent toward the ground.

> TOOMY
> Try it, you old jackass.

The plane bumps up and down again. Albert

leans over the unconscious Bethany, staring across the seats and out a window, desperately looking for a break in the clouds.

There is nothing out there but unending shades of grey streaming past the windows.

INT. COCKPIT - DAY

Nick leans forward, staring out the window at the grey as Brian brings the plane down.

The Brit seems calmer now.

                    NICK
          How low is the ceiling,
          mate?

                    BRIAN
          I don`t know. Lower than
          I`d hoped, I can tell you
          that.

Nick sits back with a dour grin.

                    NICK
          Oh, that makes me feel
          better.

Brian glances at him, cutting him a smile.

                    BRIAN
          If I get down to five
          hundred feet and there`s
          still no break in the

                    BRIAN (CONT.)
          cloud cover, I`ll take us
          up again and fly down to
          Portland.

Nick stares out the window at the unending
grey streaming past.

                    NICK
          Maybe you ought to take
          us that way now.

Brian shakes his head.

                    BRIAN
          The weather there is
          almost always worse than
          the weather here.

The plane suddenly takes another twist and
turn as it hits turbulence.

Nick clamps his hands on the armrest,
holding himself in place.

                    NICK
          This is starting to look
          like a bad decision,
          matey.

The plane strikes another invisible air
pocket, and the 767 shivers like a dog
with a bad chill.

They hear faint screams from the cabin
behind them, but there`s nothing they can
do as Brian makes a correction.

                    BRIAN
          We haven`t struck out
          yet.

He glances down at the altimeter. 2,200
feet and falling as they continue to
descend.

Nick watches him.

                    NICK
          But we _are_ running out of
          room, aren`t we? I mean,
          somewhere beneath all
          this grayness, the ground
          is rushing up to meet us,
          isn`t it?

                    BRIAN
          Yes, but --

He suddenly breaks off as outside the
window, the clouds begin to rapidly thin.
He breathes a huge sigh of relief.

                    BRIAN
          Here we are. Coming
          through.

A gauzy rip appears in the clouds. Brian
cranes his neck in his seat, looking out
the window.

EXT. PLANE - DAY

The 767 slowly leaves the cloud bank behind
as it zooms over the leaded grayness of

the Atlantic Ocean.

INT. COCKPIT - DAY

Brian picks up the microphone and speaks
into it.

> BRIAN
> We`re broken through
> the ceiling, ladies and
> gentlemen. In a few
> minutes, you`re going to
> hear a thump from below.
> That will be the landing
> gear lowering into place.
> I am continuing our
> descent into the Bangor
> area.

He clicks off and turns to Nick.

> BRIAN
> Wish me luck, Nick.

Nick looks at him like a man newly converted
and answers fervently.

> NICK
> Oh, I do, matey -- I do.

INT. MAIN CABIN - DAY

Laurel cranes her neck and looks out the
window. She catches glimpses of the ocean,
whitecaps, then a large chunk of rock
poking out of the water. They pass over a

small island and by sitting back, she can
see the coast dead ahead.

Dinah clutches at her just as they hit the
coast.

                    DINAH
          What do you see, Laurel?

                    LAUREL
          We`re over land. A field,
          a forest, what looks like
          a pond --

She suddenly lets out a small cry of
triumph. Dinah clutches her harder.

                    DINAH
          What?

                    LAUREL
          I see a narrow road
          leading into a small
          seaside village.

EXT. PLANE - DAY

More of the town slides into view
beneath the plane`s belly. From up here,
it looks like a toy village with tiny
toy cars parked along the main street.

INT. MAIN CABIN - DAY

Laurel continues to stare out the window,
seeing the town and cars and all the signs

of habitation and community flow past
below. Her voice fills with happiness.

                    LAUREL
          It`s all there, Dinah!
          It`s all there!

From the row behind her, Robert Jenkins,
who has also been looking out the window,
speaks in a voice leaden with doom.

                     BOB
          Madame, I am afraid you
          are quite wrong.

EXT. SKY - DAY

The long white jet with the American Pride
eagle printed on its tail begins its long
descent into Bangor Airport. Although
there`s no rain, the morning is gray and
sunless and the plane prints no shadow on
the ground below as it flies toward the
cluster of city ahead.

EXT. PLANE UNDERCARRIAGE - DAY

The belly of the plane slides open and the
wheels drop down below the cockpit area.

INT. COCKPIT - DAY

The plane banks slightly to the left as
Brian adjusts course, now able to correct
visually. Nick rises up out of his seat,
staring at the rapidly growing airport

ahead.

                    NICK
          I see it! I see the
          airport! My God, what a
          beautiful sight!

Brian replies without looking up, one hand
on the flight stick, the other punching
buttons on the control board.

                    BRIAN
          Buckle up! We`re coming
          in!

Nick drops back into his seat and buckles
up as Brian centers the plane`s nose on
the runway ahead and continues down the
slide. He checks his altimeter and watches
it drop from 1,000 to 800 feet. Below him
a seemingly endless pine forest passes
beneath the plane`s wings. He checks the
green lights on his flaps and picks up
the radio, trying to raise someone at the
airport.

                    BRIAN
          Bangor Tower, this is
          Flight 29. <u>I am declaring</u>
          <u>an emergency</u>. If you
          have runway traffic, get
          it out of the way. I`m
          coming in.

He glances at the airspeed indicator just
in time to see it drop below 140 m.p.h.
Nick looks out the window, sees a golf

course sweeping below, then the green of a Holiday Inn sign, and then lights which mark the end of the runway. They are not green or red; they are just dark globs sitting there.

                    NICK
          The runway lights are
          dead.

                    BRIAN
          No time to worry about it
          now.

He inclines the flight wheel further forward and the plane noses down toward the runway.

EXT. RUNWAY - DAY

The 767 hits the runway, bumps once, and comes down again.

It streaks along at a 120 miles an hour with its nose slightly up and its wings tilted at a mild angle.

INT. COCKPIT - DAY

Brian leans forward and applies full flaps and reverses the thrusters.

There is another bump as the nose grabs the runway and holds.

EXT. RUNWAY - DAY

The plane begins to slow, from a hundred and twenty to a hundred, from a hundred to eighty, then forty, finally cruising along at a speed slightly faster than a man running.

INT. COCKPIT - DAY

Brian turns to Nick with a grin.

                    BRIAN
          Routine landing. Nothing
          to it.

He gives a long, shuddery laugh and picks up the intercom mike, speaking into it.

                    BRIAN
          Ladies and gentlemen,
          welcome to Bangor.

From behind them in the main cabin they hear a chorus of whistles and cheers. Brian laughs, but Nick does not. He is leaning over Brian`s shoulder, staring out the cockpit window.

EXT. RUNWAY - DAY

Nothing moves as the 767 taxis slowly down the runway toward the main terminal.

Nothing on the grid work of runways, nothing on the taxiways.

INT. COCKPIT - DAY

Nick continues to stare out the window. He sees an Army transport plane, a C12, parked on an outer taxiway and a Delta 727 parked at one of the jet ways, but they are as still as statues.

Nick speaks softly, half to himself, half to Brian.

                    NICK
          Thank you for the welcome,
          my friend. My deep
          appreciation stems from
          the fact that it appears
          you are the only one who
          is going to extend one.
          This place is utterly,
          totally deserted.

Brian looks up at him, his face creased with a frown.

                    BRIAN
          It can`t be.

                    NICK
          Unfortunately, I`m afraid
          it is.

Brian slams on the brakes and cuts the engines.

EXT. RUNWAY - DAY

The plane glides to a halt on the silent,

empty runway.

INT. COCKPIT - DAY

Brian turns off the engines. He and Nick listen to them wind down and die. They are left with the faint whisper of the auxiliary power. Brian and Nick unbuckle their safety harnesses and stand. Nick glances at the pilot.

                    NICK
          Now what, Brian?

                    BRIAN
          We get off the plane and
          see what`s what.

He turns for the door, Nick following.

INT. MAIN CABIN - DAY

Brian and Nick stop in the main cabin, Brian looking at his eight other passengers. For a moment there is nothing but silence, than Albert lifts his hands and begins to applaud.

Bob Jenkins joins him -- and Don Gaffney -- and Laurel Stevenson. Rudy Warwick looks around and then joins in. Dinah looks blindly at Laurel, listening to the clapping.

                    DINAH
          What is it?

                    LAUREL
          It`s the Captain. It`s
          the Captain who brought
          us down safely.

She begins to cry as Dinah joins her,
clapping for Brian Engle who just stands
there, staring dumbly at them all. Behind
him, Nick joins in. The passengers unbuckle
their belts and stand in front of him,
applauding him.

All that is, except for Bethany who has
not awoken yet from her faint, and Craig
Toomy, who pans them with his strange
lunar gaze, and then begins to rip a fresh
strip of paper from an airline magazine.
Brian flushes and lifts his hands to stop
the applause, but it goes on for a moment
more before the passengers quiet down.

                    BRIAN
          Ladies and gentlemen,
          please please, I assure
          you, it was a very
          routine landing.

Bob suddenly breaks out in a very passable
Gary Cooper imitation.

                    BOB
          Shucks, ma`am -- t`wern`t
          nothin`.

Albert bursts out laughing. Beside him,
Bethany`s eyes flutter open and she looks
around, dazed.

                    BETHANY
          We got down alive, didn`t
          we? My God! That`s great!

Brian raises his arms higher, calling for
quiet.

                     BRIAN
          Please. If I could have
          your attention, please.

They stop applauding one-by-one and look
at him expectantly.

All except Toomy who suddenly unbuckles
his seat belt and rises, rummaging around
in the overhead compartment, frowning in
concentration.

Brian continues, trying to ignore him.

                     BRIAN
          You`ve looked out the
          windows, so you know as
          much as I do. Not only
          have all the passengers
          and crew on this flight
          disappeared, but it now
          looks like the people
          on the ground have
          disappeared as well
          -- but logic suggests
          that since we survived
          whatever-it-was, others
          must have survived it as
          well.

In a side seat, Bob shakes his head, murmuring to himself.

> BOB
> False logic.

Albert looks across the aisle from his seat next to Bethany, his brow creasing as he catches the words.

Brian continues his talk.

> BRIAN
> The best way to deal with
> this, I think, is to take
> things one step at a
> time. Step one is exiting
> the plane.

Craig Toomy, briefcase from the overhead rack now firmly in hand, looks at Brian, speaking in a disconcertingly calm tone.

> TOOMY
> I bought a ticket to
> Boston. Boston is where I
> want to go.

Nick steps out from behind Brian and raises one hand, his fingers curled in against his palm, and scissors two of his knuckles together in a nose-pinching gesture.

Toomy gets the message and clamps his mouth shut. Brian continues.

                    BRIAN
          We`ll have to use the
          emergency slide, so
          I want to review the
          procedures with you.
          Listen carefully, then
          form a single-file line
          behind me --

EXT. 767 - DAY

The escape slide, a large, ribbed, orange
air mattress extends at a sloping outward
angle from the open forward door of the
plane to the ground. The small group is
gathered on the ground below, watching as
Brian, the last to come, leaps into the
slide, shoes in hand, and scoots to the
bottom. Nick helps him to his feet as Brian
looks around at the deserted terminal.

                    BRIAN
          Well, here we are at
          last.

Nick sniffs the air with a sudden frown.

                    NICK
          There`s something wrong
          with the air out here.

Brian looks at him worriedly.

                    BRIAN
          What do you mean?
          Poisoned?

                    NICK
          No -- at least I don`t
          think so. But it has no
          smell, no odor.

Brian sniffs. From his expression it is
obvious his nose is telling him the same
thing. Bethany and the others look at them,
reading the growing unease in their faces.

                  BETHANY
          Is there something wrong?
          I mean, I`m not sure I
          really want to know, but
          --

Brian shakes his head, trying to be
reassuring.

                    BRIAN
          Honey, there`s nothing
          wrong here --

Dinah cuts in, her voice urgent and filled
with worry.

                    DINAH
          But there is. This place
          smells wrong. Really
          badly wrong.

ACT 5

EXT. RUNWAY - DAY

Nick drops to one knee in front of the
little blind girl.

> NICK
>
> Honey, we have to
> investigate. We don`t have
> a choice. You understand
> that, don`t you?

Dinah turns the shades of her dark glasses
toward him, her face tight with fear.

> DINAH
>
> Why? Why do we have to?
> There`s no one here.

Nick rises, exchanging a helpless glance
with Laurel.

> NICK
>
> Well, we won`t really
> know that until we check,
> will we?

> DINAH
>
> I know already. There`s
> nothing to smell and
> nothing to hear. Listen.
> No birds singing, no
> motors revving, no
> nothing. But, but --

Dinah stops, cocking her ear as though listening.

                    LAUREL
          But what, Dinah?

Dinah thinks of saying more, but then changes her mind.

She shakes her head.

                    DINAH
          Never mind.

Nick steps into the silence, looking at Brian.

                    NICK
          What now, Captain?

                    BRIAN
          You tell me. Us. I
          suspect this is more your
          territory than mine.

Nick looks at him to see if he really means to turn control of the group over to him.

Brian nods, signalling he does as Craig Toomy suddenly breaks in, addressing Brian.

                    TOOMY
          You know I`m going to
          report you for this,
          don`t you? You know I

                    TOOMY (CONT.)
          plan to sue this entire
          airline for thirty
          million dollars, and that
          I plan to name you as
          primary respondent.

                    BRIAN
          That`s your privilege,
          Mr. -- ?

                    TOOMY
          Toomy. Craig Toomy.

                    BRIAN
          -- Mr. Toomy.
                    (a beat, then)
          Mr. Toomy, are you aware
          of what has happened to
          us?

Toomy turns, looking for a moment at the totally deserted tarmac and the wide, slightly polarized terminal windows where no happy friends and relatives wait to greet arriving passengers and his mind can no longer deal with it.

He falls into the deep well of his insanity.

INT. CRAIG TOOMY`S CHILDHOOD ROOM - NIGHT (IN HIS MIND)

A red-faced RODGER TOOMY, 40 plus, looms over his 9 year old son, CRAIG, staring down at him furiously.

He waves a report card in front of the boy`s face, screaming at him.

> ROGER
> This is terrible, just terrible! An A minus and a B! A "B", for God`s sakes! What do you want to do, dig ditches for the rest of your life?!

Nine year old Craig looks up at his father. Tears spring into his eyes.

> CRAIG
> N-N-No.

> ROGER
> Well, then you`d better get on the stick and get all A`s. Or you know what will happen to you, don`t you?

He bends over the boy, staring down at him with his furious red-face, waiting impatiently for an answer.

> CRAIG
> Y-Y-Yes. The <u>Langoliers</u> will get me.

> ROGER
> That`s right. And you know what the Langoliers do to lazy, time-wasting little boys, don`t you?

Little Craig looks up at his red-faced father, now absolutely terrified.

> CRAIG
> T-T-they eat them?

> ROGER
> That`s right. They <u>eat</u> them!

Roger Toomy breaks into a hearty LAUGH filled with sadistic glee, just LAUGHING and LAUGHING as the little boy stares up at him, terrified.

A voice intrudes OVER.

> BRIAN (V.O.)
> Mr. Toomy? Mr. Toomy, are you listening to me.

EXT. RUNWAY - DAY (BACK INTO REALITY)

Toomy snaps out of it and turns to Brian, looking at him with utter seriousness.

> TOOMY
> Of course, and I know what happened to everybody here. The Langoliers got them.

> BRIAN
> Pardon me?

Toomy switches the subject without missing a beat.

                    TOOMY
          Do you know how important
          my meeting at the
          Prudential Center in
          Boston is? The economic
          fate of nations may hinge
          upon the result of that
          meeting. A meeting from
          which I shall be absent.

                    BRIAN
          Mr. Toomy, that`s all
          very interesting, but I
          really don`t have time --

Toomy suddenly explodes, screaming at him.
It freezes everyone.

                    TOOMY
          <u>Time</u>! What in the hell
          do <u>you</u> know about time?
          Ask me! I know <u>all</u> about
          time! Time is short, sir!
          <u>Time is short as hell</u>!

Nick steps protectively in front of Brian.
Toomy snaps his mouth shut and steps back.
His face goes blank. Nick turns back to
Brian.

                    NICK
          What would be the
          quickest way inside?

Brian nods toward a line of baggage trains
parked beneath the overhang of the main
terminal.

                    BRIAN
          I guess through that
          luggage conveyor.

Nick turns to the rest of the group,
raising his voice.

                    NICK
          All right, let`s hike
          on over, ladies and
          gentlemen, shall we?

They all start forward, Laurel taking
Dinah`s hand. She looks down at her as
they walk.

                    LAUREL
          You shouldn`t worry
          so much, Dinah. It`s
          just that the situation
          is strange. Therefore
          everything seems strange.

                    DINAH
          Including the sound your
          high heels make hitting
          the concrete?

Laurel cracks an ear, listening to the
sound of her heels on the tarmac. Dinah
is right. They sound odd somehow. She
tightens her grip on the girl`s hand.

                    LAUREL
          You`re right. They sound
          --

                    DINAH
          Weak?

                    LAUREL
          That`s right. Weak.
          Almost like they don`t
          have any strength.

The group comes to a halt before a dead
conveyor belt which carries luggage into
the terminal through a hole covered with
hanging strips of rubber. The conveyor
makes a wide circle on the apron, then
re-enters the terminal through another
hole hung with rubber strips. Nick boosts
himself onto the conveyor belt and walks
down to one of the holes. When he gets
there, he drops to his knees and pokes his
head through. The other nine people watch
him. After a moment he withdraws his head,
looking at them with forced cheerfulness.

                    NICK
          Coast`s clear.

With that Nick disappears through the
hole. Brian turns, helping Laurel and
Dinah. Dinah pauses just outside the hole,
looking back toward Laurel.

                    DINAH
          It`s really wrong here.

With that she turns and disappears through
the hole. Laurel, Brian, and the others
follow.

INT. MAIN TERMINAL - DAY

One by one they emerge into the terminal, Albert helping Dinah off the conveyor belt. They all stand there, looking around in silent wonder. The rental-car stalls are deserted. The ARRIVALS-DEPARTURES monitors are dark and dead. No one stands at the bank of counters serving Delta, United, Northwest Air-Link, or Mid-Coast Airways.

The huge tank in the middle of the floor with the BUY MAINE LOBSTERS banner stretched across it is full of water, but there are no lobsters in it. The overhead fluorescents are off, and the small amount of light entering through the doors on the far side of the large room peters out halfway across the floor, leaving the little group from Flight 29 huddled together in an unpleasant nest of shadows. Nick rubs his hands together, trying for briskness but only managing unease.

                    NICK
          Right, then. Let`s try
          the telephones, shall we?

He heads for a bank of phones as Albert wanders over to the Budget Rent-A-Car desk. It looks like the clerk just stepped away for a minute, the slots in the rear wall full of rental agreements waiting for arriving passengers. Suddenly there is a dry crunching noise behind him. He whirls, bringing his violin case up like

a cudgel, only to find himself facing
Bethany, just touching a match to the tip
of her cigarette.

She grins.

> BETHANY
> Scare you?

> ALBERT
> A little.

He lowers his violin case as Bethany shakes
out the match and drops it, taking a deep
drag on her smoke.

> BETHANY
> Gawd -- at least that`s
> better. I didn`t dare
> to on the plane. I was
> afraid something might
> blow up.

Bob leaves the slowly diminishing group
and strolls over.

> BOB
> You know, I quit those
> about ten years ago

Bethany raises a hand.

> BETHANY
> No lectures, please. I`ve
> already had enough to
> last me a lifetime.

                    BOB
          Actually, I was going to
          ask if I could have one.

Bethany smiles and offers him one of her
smokes. Bob takes it and she lights it for
him. He inhales, than coughs out a series
of smoke-signal puffs.

She grins.

                  BETHANY
          You have been away.

Bob nods.

                    BOB
          But I`ll get used to it
          in a hurry, I`m afraid.
          What time does your watch
          say, Albert?

Albert checks his wristwatch.

                  ALBERT
          Quarter to nine.

Bob glances at his watch.

                    BOB
          Mine, too, but I don`t
          trust it. It feels later
          to me than that.

Albert thinks about it, looks around, then
back at Bob.

                    ALBERT
You know, it <u>does</u>. It
feels like it`s almost
lunchtime. Isn`t that
nuts?

                    BETHANY
It`s not nuts. It`s just
jet lag.

                     BOB
I disagree. We traveled
West to East, young lady.
Any temporal dislocation
west-east travelers feel
goes the other way. They
feel it`s <u>earlier</u> than it
should be.

                    ALBERT
I wanted to ask you
something about that
on the plane. When the
captain told us there
must be other people
here, you said "false
logic." But it seems
straight enough to me.
We were all asleep, and
<u>we`re</u> here. And if this
happened at -
      (nods at the wall clock, which has
            stopped dead)
4:07, Bangor time, almost
everybody in town must
have been asleep.

                    BOB
          Yes. So where are they?

Albert looks around the too empty terminal,
trying to find an answer.

                  ALBERT
          Well --

A sudden BANG turns them around to see
Nick forcibly hanging up one of the pay
phones. It is the last in a long line and
he has tried everyone of them. He looks
across the terminal at the others.

                  NICK
          It`s a washout. They`re
          all dead. The coin fed
          ones as well as the
          direct dials. You can add
          the sound of no phones
          ringing to that of no
          dogs barking, Brian.

He rejoins the group as do Albert, Dinah,
and Bob. Although none of them notice,
Craig Toomy is no longer there. Beside
Laurel, Dinah turns in small circles like
a human radar dish, scoping the place out.
Laurel looks at the group.

                  LAUREL
          So what do we do now?

They all look at each other, momentarily
without an answer. Rudy Warwick, the bald
businessman, steps in.

                    RUDY
          Let`s go upstairs. That`s
          where the restaurant must
          be.

They all look at him. Gaffney snorts.

                    GAFFNEY
          You`ve got a one-track
          mind, mister.

Rudy looks at him from under one raised
eyebrow.

                    RUDY
          First, the name is Rudy
          Warwick, not mister.
          Second, people think
          better when their
          stomachs are full. It`s
          just a law of nature.

                    BOB
          I think Mr. Warwick is
          quite right. We all <u>could</u>
          use something to eat.

Nick shrugs. He suddenly looks tired and
confused.

                    NICK
          Why not? I`m starting to
          feel like Mr. Robinson
          Bloody Crusoe.

The little group starts toward the
escalator, which like everything else in

the terminal, is dead.

Albert, Bethany, and Bob walk together,
toward the rear.

Albert cuts a look at Bob.

> ALBERT
> You know something, don`t
> you?

> BOB
> I <u>might</u>. Then again I
> might not. But I do have
> a suggestion.
> (to Bethany)
> Save your matches.

> BETHANY
> I don`t get what you
> mean. There`s probably
> a news-stand upstairs,
> Mr. Jenkins. They`ll
> have lots of matches.
> Disposable lighters, too.

> BOB
> I agree, but I still
> advise you to save your
> matches.

Brian suddenly jerks to halt at the foot
of the dead escalator, his eyes scanning
the little group of refugees.

> BRIAN
> Where`s Mr. Toomy?

                    GAFFNEY
          Who cares? Good riddance
          to bad rubbish.

Brian glances at Nick. Nick shrugs.

                     NICK
          Didn`t see him go, mate.
          Sorry.

Brian raises his head and shouts into the
vast space of the dead, empty terminal.

                    BRIAN
          Toomy! Craig Toomy! Where
          are you?

There is no response. Only that queer,
oppressive silence. They all look around,
strangely uneasy. Rudy is the first to
break the silence.

                    RUDY
          Something`s wrong.

They all look at each other. They know
he`s right, but they don`t know why.
Laurel suddenly breaks the silence with
an answer.

                    LAUREL
          There`s no echo.

                   GAFFNEY
          What do you mean? That`s
          impossible.

Laurel raises her head, calling out.

                    LAUREL
          HELLO? IS ANYBODY THERE?

Her voice dies almost immediately, the echo swallowed up before it can begin. They all look at each other, trying to suppress a growing feeling of horror and failing.

ACT 6

INT. SECOND-FLOOR CENTRAL WAITING ROOM - DAY

Craig Toomy strides briskly across the large, empty waiting room, his briefcase swinging beside his right knee. At the far end, a sign hangs over the mouth of a wide, dark corridor.

It reads "GATE 5; INTERNATIONAL ARRIVALS; DUTY FREE SHOPS, U.S. CUSTOMS; AIRPORT SECURITY."

He heads in that direction only to glance out one of the large, side windows. There is nothing to see but the empty concrete and the motionless white sky, but his eyes begin to widen and he comes to a slow halt, staring out the window. Then a voice whispers behind him.

> ROGER TOOMY (O.S.)
> They`re coming, son. The
> Langoliers are coming.

Toomy turns to see his father sitting in one of the waiting room chairs, reading a Wall Street Journal. He doesn`t seem a day older than he did in Toomy`s memory of him as a nine year old child.

> TOOMY
> No. No one is coming.

                    ROGER TOOMY
          Yes, they are. And
          they`re coming for <u>you</u> if
          you don`t get to Boston
          and explain what happened
          to all that money.

                    TOOMY
          They`re going to fire me.

                    ROGER TOOMY
          No, they won`t. Make
          up an excuse. The bond
          trader lied to you about
          the market --

                    TOOMY
          I knew the bonds were
          going to crash.

His father stares at him, stunned by this
revelation.

                    ROGER TOOMY
          What?

Toomy nods.

                    TOOMY
          I bought them
          deliberately. I can`t
          take it anymore, father,
          always having to get
          ahead, kill or be killed,
          the incessant pressure --

Roger Toomy rises and comes to stand beside

his son at the window.

                    ROGER TOOMY
          You can`t tell them that.
          They will fire you.

Toomy nods enthusiastically.

                    TOOMY
          Yes. Yes, I`ll be free at
          last --

Roger Toomy`s face hardens into a rock
like mask.

                    ROGER TOOMY
          You`ll make excuses, do
          you hear me. Do it right,
          they`ll believe you.

Toomy steps back fearfully, shaking his
head.

                    TOOMY
          No. No, I won't

                    ROGER TOOMY
          If you don`t, <u>they`ll</u> get
          you.

He turns, nodding eastward out the window.
Instant fear floods Toomy`s eyes.

                    TOOMY
          No, they won`t. They
          don`t even exist --

                    ROGER TOOMY
              Yes, they do. And you
              know it. Now, you will do
              as I say -- or face <u>them</u>.

Toomy`s gaze is still fixed out the window,
his face a mask of insane fear. He licks
his dry lips, suddenly nodding wildly.

                      TOOMY
              All right, father, I`ll
              do whatever you want.
              Just don`t let them get
              me --

He turns from the window to look at his
father, but his father is no longer there.
No one is.

Toomy slowly backs away, then turns and runs
down the darkened corridor, disappearing
from sight.

INT. CORRIDOR - DAY

He passes the empty shops without a glance.
Beyond them he comes to the door he was
looking for, a small rectangular plaque
mounted on it just above a bull`s-eye
peep-hole. It says "AIRPORT SECURITY." He
slips inside.

INT. CENTRAL WAITING ROOM - DAY

The small group, led by Brian and Nick,
reach the top of the stalled escalator to
find themselves in BIA`s central waiting

room. It is a large square box filled with contoured plastic seats, and dominated by a wall of large polarized windows (the same windows Craig Toomy was staring out just moments earlier). Nick starts for the corridor leading to the Airport Security Office and the International Arrivals Annex.

                    NICK
          Come on --

Dinah suddenly speaks up in a strong, urgent voice.

                    DINAH
          Wait.

They all stop and turn toward her curiously. Dinah drops Laurel`s hand and cups her thumbs behind her ears and splays her fingers like fans.

She turns slowly toward the huge windows and takes off her glasses, staring out the glass with dark brown eyes.

She stands there, still as a post, listening with all her might. Brian watches her.

                    BRIAN
          What --

                    DINAH
          Shhh -- I hear something.

She walks toward the windows as the others

stand there, now listening as hard as they
can.

Brian slowly shakes his head.

                    BRIAN
          There`s nothing out there.
          It`s your imagination,
          that`s all.

                    LAUREL
          I wouldn`t be so sure --

She turns her gaze to Dinah as the girl
comes to a halt, staring blindly out the
window.

                    LAUREL
          What? What do you hear,
          Dinah?

                    DINAH
          I don`t know. It`s very
          faint. I heard it when
          we got off the airplane,
          and then I decided it
          was just my imagination.
          Now I can hear it even
          through the glass. It
          sounds -- a little like
          Rice Krispies after you
          pour in the milk.

Brian turns to Nick, speaking in a low
voice.

                    BRIAN
          Do you hear anything?

                    NICK
          Not a bloody thing. But
          she`s blind. She`s used
          to making her ears do
          double duty.

Brian leans in even closer to Nick, his
lips almost touching the Brit`s ears.

                    BRIAN
          I think it`s hysteria.

Dinah turns from the window, looking in
their direction.

She speaks, mimicking them almost
perfectly.

                    DINAH
          Do you hear anything? Not
          a bloody thing. But she`s
          blind. She`s used to
          making her ears do double
          duty.
               (a beat, then)
          I think it`s hysteria.

The two men stare at the girl, momentarily
at a loss for words.

Laurel steps in.

                    LAUREL
          Dinah, what are you

                    LAUREL (CONT.)
          talking about?

                    BRIAN
          I was talking to Nick.
          She heard us from over
          there by the window.

Laurel looks at the distance between the
two men and the young girl standing by the
window.

It`s at least twenty feet, and the two men
were speaking in hushed whispers. Bethany
looks at Dinah and shakes her head in
admiration.

                    BETHANY
          You`ve got great ears,
          hon.

                    DINAH
          I hear what I hear. And I
          hear something out there.
          In that direction.

She points due east through the glass, her
unseeing eyes sweeping them.

                    DINAH
          And it`s <u>awful</u>. A really
          terrible, scary sound.

                    GAFFNEY
          If you knew what it was,
          little miss, that would
          help.

She puts her dark glasses on with a trembling hand.

                    DINAH
          I don`t. But I know it`s
          closer than it was. We
          have to get out of here.
          And soon.

                    BRIAN
          Dinah, the plane we came
          in on is almost out of
          fuel --

Dinah suddenly screams at him shrilly.

                    DINAH
          <u>Then you have to put some
          more in it</u>! It`s <u>coming</u>,
          don`t you understand?
          It`s <u>coming</u>, and if we
          haven`t gone by the time
          it gets here, <u>we`re all
          going to die</u>!

Her voice cracks and she begins to sob. She staggers toward them, her self-possession utterly gone. Laurel grabs her before she can stumble over one of the guide ropes which mark the way to the security check point and hugs her tightly, looking helplessly at the others in their small group. They look back at her just as helplessly.

INT. AIRPORT SECURITY OFFICE - DAY

Craig Toomy yanks open a locker with the name MARKEY Dymotaped to the front. Hanging from a hook next to a security guard`s uniform is a holster with the butt of a service revolver protruding. Toomy unsnaps the safety strap and takes out the gun. He fumbles the cylinder open and inspects the chambers. All six are filled with bullets. He freezes, staring at them as his father`s VOICE echoes inside his head.

>   ROGER TOOMY (V.O.)
>   Don`t forget, Craiggy-
>   weggy. The Langoliers
>   were here, and they will
>   be back. You better be
>   gone when they get here
>   -- or you know what will
>   happen.

Craig nods gravely, his eyes spinning like pin-wheels in a hurricane as he speaks to himself aloud.

>   TOOMY
>   Yes. I know. They`ll eat
>   me. They`ll eat me all
>   up.

He collapses in a chair before a formica table and grabs the nearest duty roster. His fingers find the edge and he pulls down. <u>Riii--ip</u>!

INT. CENTRAL WAITING ROOM - DAY

The frozen silence following Dinah's warning is finally broken by Nick who looks at Brian.

> NICK
>> There's a 727 out there, all cozied up to a jet way. Can you fly one of those?

> BRIAN
>> Yes.

Nick spreads his hands as thought to say, "Well, there we go." Bob steps in.

> BOB
>> There's a slight problem. Assuming we do take off again, exactly where should we go?

Dinah answers immediately.

> DINAH
>> Away. Away from that sound.

Bob turns to her.

> BOB
>> How long before it gets here, Dinah? Do you have any idea at all?

                    DINAH
          No. I think it`s still
          far, but --

Bob cuts her off, rubbing his hands
together briskly.

                    BOB
          Well, then I suggest we
          do exactly as Mr. Warwick
          has suggested. Let`s step
          over to the restaurant,
          have a bite to eat, and
          discuss what happens
          next.

He strikes off across the room toward the
Cloud Nine restaurant without waiting for
the others. They stare after him, then at
each other.

                    GAFFNEY
          Who elected him the
          leader of the group?

Albert turns to Gaffney and the others.

                    ALBERT
          We better go along. I
          think he really knows his
          stuff.

                    BRIAN
          What kind of stuff?

                    ALBERT
          I don`t know exactly, but

                    ALBERT (CONT.)
          I have a feeling it`s
          worth finding out.

Albert follows Bob, Bethany following him.
The others exchange glances and follow,
Laurel leading Dinah by the hand.

The little girl is very, very pale.

INT. CLOUD NINE RESTAURANT - DAY

The restaurant is really a cafeteria with
a cold-case full of drinks and sandwiches
at the rear and a stainless steel counter
in front. The side facing the terminal is
open, roped off by a velvet cord. Bob is
standing by the cash register as Albert
and Bethany enter.

                    BOB
          May I have another
          cigarette, Bethany?

                    BETHANY
          Gee, you`re a real mooch.

She smiles and hands him a cigarette,
following it with a book of matches.

He takes the cigarette, but refuses the
matches, reaching for a bowlful of them on
the counter beside the cash register.

                    BOB
          I`ll just use one of
          these if that`s all right

                    BOB (CONT.)
          with you.

Bethany watches as he pulls one of the
match books from the bowl, and detaches a
paper match.

                    BETHANY
          Sure, but why?

                    BOB
          That`s what we`re going
          to find out.

The others have entered the room by now
and gather around him, all except Rudy,
that is, who has drifted to the rear of
the service area, and is inspecting the
contents of the cold case. Bob tries to
strike the match, but nothing happens. He
tries again and again, but still nothing
happens. He shakes his head.

                    BOB
          Son of a bee. We seem
          to have discovered yet
          another problem. May
          I borrow your book of
          matches, Bethany?

She hands it over without a word. Nick and
the others watch.

                    NICK
          Wait a minute, matey.
          Exactly what do you know?

                    BOB
          Only that this situation
          has even wider
          implications than we
          at first thought. And
          I have an idea that we
          all may have made one
          big mistake. An error of
          perspective, I`d call it.

As he talks, Rudy wanders back toward
them. He has selected a wrapped sandwich
and a bottle of beer. They seem to have
cheered him a lot.

                    RUDY
          What`s happening, folks?

                    BRIAN
          I`ll be damned if I know,
          but I don`t like it much.

Bob pulls one of the matches from Bethany`s
book and strikes it. It lights immediately.
He uses it to light his cigarette, and
then holds the lit match under the book
from the bowl by the cash register. He
plays the flame back and forth underneath
the heads of the other matches, but they
don`t light. The others watch, fascinated.
Finally there`s a sickly <u>phsss</u> SOUND and
a few of the matches erupt into dull,
momentary life before they gutter out. Bob
smiles grimly.

                    BOB
          Even that is more than I

                    BOB (CONT.)
     expected.

                      BRIAN
          All right. Tell us about
          it. I know --

At that moment Rudy snorts with disgust,
and they all turn, looking at him. He had
unwrapped his sandwich and taken a large
bite. Now he spits it out onto the floor
with a grimace of disgust.

                      RUDY
          It`s spoiled. Oh,
          goddamn, I hate that!

Bob cocks an eyebrow.

                      BOB
          Spoiled? Oh, I doubt
          that. We know by the
          clocks that the power in
          the cold case went out
          less than five hours ago.

                      RUDY
          Here, if you don`t think
          it`s spoiled, you try it.

He holds the sandwich out to Bob. The
older man takes it, screws up his courage,
and bites down. An expression of disgust
sweeps his face, but he keeps on chewing.
Once, twice, then spits into a trash bin
below the condiments shelf and drops the
rest of the sandwich after it.

                    BOB
          Not spoiled. Tasteless.
          Like chewing paper. No
          wonder you thought it was
          spoiled.

Rudy replies stubbornly.

                    RUDY
          It _was_ spoiled.

                    BOB
          Try your beer. That
          should be all right.

Rudy looks thoughtfully at the bottle of
Budweiser in his hand, then shakes his
head, and offers the beer to Bob.

                    RUDY
          I don`t want it anymore.

Don Gaffney suddenly speaks up, stepping
forward.

                    GAFFNEY
          Here, give it to me. I`ve
          drunk 'em warm before and
          they don`t cross my eyes
          none.

He takes the beer, twists off the cap, and
upends it, taking a mouthful. A second
later he whirls and spits the beer on the
floor.

                    GAFFNEY
           <u>Jesus</u>! Flat! Flat and
           tasteless as an old tire!

Bob brightens.

                      BOB
           Is it? Good! Great!
           Something we can all see!

He grabs glasses from the counter with
both hands, others falling and shattering
on the floor. Bob pays no heed as he sets
them out along the counter with the speed
of a practiced bartender, yelling at
Bethany and Albert.

                      BOB
           Bring me some more beer.
           And a couple of soft
           drinks, while you`re at
           it.

The teenagers go to the cold-case, each
taking four or five bottles, picking at
random.

INT. SECURITY OFFICE - DAY

Craig Toomy tears the last of the duty
rooster into a strip and lets it flutter to
the floor at his feet where another three
dozen lie. His father`s voice suddenly
speaks to him.

                 ROGER TOOMY (V.O.)
           You can`t dilly-dally any

                    ROGER TOOMY (CONT.)
          longer, Craigy-weggy. You
          have to get to Boston and
          you have to do it now!

Craig abruptly rises, picks up his
briefcase and gun and heads for the door.

INT. CORRIDOR - DAY

He comes out the door and down the corridor,
walking for the main waiting room. Inside
his head, he rehearses what he`s going to
say to the other passengers when he sees
them.

                    CRAIG TOOMY (V.O.)
          I don`t want to shoot
          you, but I will if I have
          to. I don`t want to shoot
          you, but I will if I have
          to.

He suddenly speaks out loud in a crazed,
singsong voice.

                    TOOMY
          I will if I have to. I
          will if I have to.

ACT 7

INT. WAITING ROOM - DAY

He enters the huge room, spots the group in the cafeteria, and walks in their direction.

His finger finds the hammer of the gun and he cocks it back. Halfway across the room, his attention is once more snared by the pallid light coming through the window, and he turns in that direction.

He walks slowly to the window, staring out, ignoring the murmur of the other passengers behind him as he mumbles to himself with a shudder.

> TOOMY
>> You`re out there, aren`t you? But I`ll be gone by the time you get here. I`ll be gone --

INT. CLOUD NINE RESTAURANT - DAY

Bob pours a little from each bottle of beer and soda into its own glass. They are all equally flat. Nick looks at Bob.

> NICK
>> All right, they`re all flat. But why?

                    BOB
          I have an idea. But
          before I say anything
          else, I want you to look
          around this place and
          tell me what`s different
          about it than the plane.

They all look around, concentrating so
fiercely on the little cluster of chairs
and tables nearby that nobody notices
Craig Toomy standing on the far side of
the waiting room -- gazing out one of the
huge windows at the tarmac below. Then
understanding dawns in Albert`s eyes and
a huge smile lights up his face.

                  ALBERT
          The rings! The purses!
          The wallets! The surgical
          pins! None of that stuff
          is here!

Bob turns to Albert with a smile of his
own. Over his shoulder, Craig Toomy starts
to move in their direction, picking up
speed as he comes.

                    BOB
          Correct. One hundred
          percent correct. As you
          say, none of that stuff
          is here. But it was on
          the airplane when we
          survivors woke up, so why
          isn`t it here?

                    RUDY
          Maybe nobody was here
          when it happened.

                    BOB
          Nonsense. An airport is
          like a police or fire
          station. There are always
          people around, regardless
          of the hour.

Albert stares at him, suddenly awe-struck
as he realizes where Bob is headed. Behind
him, Toomy is getting closer, moving almost
at a run now.

                    ALBERT
          You think we`ve flown
          into another dimension,
          don`t you? Just like in a
          science fiction story.

Dinah suddenly cocks her head, listening
hard as Bob replies.

                    BOB
          No, I think --

Dinah cries out.

                    DINAH
          Watch out! I hear some --

Craig Toomy leaps across the velvet cord
separating the cafeteria from the terminal
and breaks through the small group before
they can move. He snaps a forearm around

Bethany`s throat and drags her backward.
He points the gun at her temple. The girl
utters a desperate, terrorized scream
as Toomy stares at the others, his eyes
shooting glances of terrified, paranoid
intelligence in every direction.

                    TOOMY
          Take me to Boston! Do
          you hear me? Take me to
          Boston!

Bethany squirms under Toomy`s restraining
forearm, fighting for breath.

                    BETHANY
          You`re choking me!
          Please, stop <u>choking</u> me!

Brian takes a step forward to help. Nick
places a hand against his chest, stopping
him without shifting his eyes from Toomy.

                    NICK
          Steady down, mate. Our
          friend here is quite
          bonkers.

Dinah blindly stares at the two of them,
trying to figure out what is going on.

                    DINAH
          What`s happening? What is
          it?

Bethany continues to squirm. Toomy tightens
his hold on her throat, yelling at her.

                    TOOMY
          Stop that! Stop moving
          around!

He digs the muzzle of the gun into the
side of her head. Nick yells at Bethany.

                    NICK
          Quit it, girl! Quit
          fighting!

Behind Toomy, Albert changes his grip
on his violin case and slowly begins to
raise it. The madman does not notice. His
eyes are shuttling rapidly back and forth
between Brian and Nick, his hands quite
literally full, holding on to Bethany.

                    TOOMY
          I don`t want to shoot
          her, but --

Bethany suddenly bucks against him, forcing
his arm upward. At the same time she socks
her behind into his crotch and sinks her
teeth into his wrist. Toomy screams.

                    TOOMY
          Ow! OWWW!

His grip loosens.

Bethany ducks under it.

Toomy points the gun at her, his face a
grimace of pain, about to shoot. Albert
leaps forward, his violin case raised.

Nick sees him lunging and bawls out.

                    NICK
          No, Albert!

Toomy sees Albert coming and shifts the
muzzle of his gun toward him, and pulls
the trigger. Instead of an explosion there
is a small pop like the sound of an old
Daisy air rifle. Albert is hit, but not
before he brings his violin case crashing
down on Toomy`s head. Toomy`s knees come
instantly unhinged and he goes down like
an express elevator. The teenager stands
there, looking at the others, his mouth
turned up in a stunned, slightly confused
smile.

                   ALBERT
          I think I have been shot.

His eyes roll back in his head and he
starts to crumple. Brian leaps forward,
grabbing him. He lowers him to the floor,
kneeling by his side and lightly slapping
his face. Bethany kneels on the other
side, staring at Albert with shining my-
hero eyes. Nick squats nearby, searching
the floor for something.

                   BRIAN
          Are you all right, kid?
          Are you all right?

Albert slowly cracks an eye, looking up at
him dazed.

                    ALBERT
          How bad am I hit? Were
          you able to stop the
          bleeding?

Nick squats beside Albert. His face wears
a bemused smile.

                    NICK
          I think you`ll live,
          matey. Hold out your
          hand and I`ll give you a
          souvenir.

Albert holds out his hand, trying to stop
it from shaking, and Nick drops something
into it. Albert holds it up to his eyes
and sees it is a bullet.

                    NICK
          I picked it up off the
          floor. It must have hit
          you square in the chest
          and then bounced off.

Albert replies weakly.

                    ALBERT
          I was thinking of the
          matches. I sort of
          thought it wouldn`t fire
          at all.

Bob peers down at him, his face very
white. He looks as if he might pass out in
another few seconds.

                    BOB
          That was very brave and
          very foolish, my boy. My
          God, what if I`d been
          wrong?

Brian reaches out a hand, helping Albert
to his feet.

                   BRIAN
          You almost were. There
          was just enough pop to
          drive the bullet out of
          the muzzle. A little more
          pop and Albert would have
          had a bullet in his lung.

Another wave of dizziness sweeps Albert and
he wavers on his feet. Bethany immediately
slips an arm around his waist. She looks
up at Albert with shining eyes.

                  BETHANY
          I thought it was really
          brave. I mean <u>incredible</u>.

Albert smiles shyly at her.

                  ALBERT
          Thanks. It wasn`t much.

Then he remembers his violin and bends
down to retrieve it. There is a deep dent
in one side and one of the catches is
sprung and bent. He opens it and looks
inside. The instrument looks all right
and he lets out a sigh. Then he thinks of

Craig Toomy and alarm replaces relief.

                    ALBERT
          Say, I didn`t kill that
          guy, did I? I hit him
          pretty hard.

He looks toward Craig Toomy laying on the
restaurant floor, unmoving, Don Gaffney
kneeling beside him. Albert suddenly feels
like passing out again. Gaffney looks up
at him and the group.

                    GAFFNEY
          He`s alive, but he`s out
          like a light.

Nick joins Gaffney, kneeling beside the
unconscious Toomy and taking his pulse.

                    NICK
          His pulse is strong and
          regular. He`ll wake up in
          a few minutes with nothing
          but a bad headache. In
          the meantime, it might
          be prudent to take a few
          precautions.

Nick rises, grabs one of the velvet ropes
that divide the restaurant from the main
terminal, and kneels beside Craig Toomy
again.

He puts the center of the rope in his
mouth, and uses his hands to flip Craig
over.

He pulls the man`s arms out from under him and brings his wrists together at the small of his back. Toomy cries out and his eyelids flutter. Laurel reacts.

> LAUREL
> Do you have to be so
> <u>rough</u>!

Nick stops, looking up at her sharply.

> NICK
> Yes, if you want him
> safely secured. You do
> want that, don`t you?

Laurel reluctantly nods.

Nick returns to Toomy, wrapping the rope twice around his lower forearms and then knotting it tightly.

Toomy`s elbows flap, and he utters a strange weak scream.

> NICK
> There! Trussed as
> neatly as Father John`s
> Christmas Turkey.

He rises, sits on the edge of a table, and looks at Bob.

> NICK
> Now what were you saying
> before we were so rudely
> interrupted?

Bob looks at him, dazed and unbelieving.

                    BOB
        What? You want me to --
        just go on? As if nothing
        had happened?

Toomy suddenly rocks on the floor, bellowing out.

                    TOOMY
        Let me up! Let me up
        right now! I demand that
        you --

Nick then does something that shocks them all.

He drives a short hard kick into Toomy`s ribs.

He pulls it at the last bit, but Toomy still utters a pained grunt and shuts up.

                    NICK
        Start again, mate, and
        I`ll stave them in.

Don Gaffney cries out, bewildered.

                    GAFFNEY
        Hey! What did you do that
        for --

Nick cuts him off, his voice vibrating with anger and urgency.

                    NICK
          Listen to me! You need
          waking up, fellows and
          girls, and I haven`t the
          time to do it gently.
          Dinah says she hears
          something coming our way,
          and I believe her. Now
          understanding what it is
          may not save our lives,
          but I`m rapidly becoming
          convinced that the lack
          of it may end them, and
          soon. Anybody disagree?

They all fall quiet and his gaze shifts
back to Bob.

                    NICK
          All right, then. Mr.
          Jenkins, please go on.

He looks at Bob who blinks owlishly at
him, still trying to stop his trembling
hands.

                    BOB
          I`m -- er -- sorry. It`s
          just that I write about
          these things. I don`t
          actually take part in
          them. Until now that is.

                    DINAH
          I think you`re doing
          great, Mr. Jenkins. And I
          like listening to you,

                    DINAH (CONT.)
          too. It makes me feel
          better.

Bob looks at her gratefully and smiles.

                    BOB
          Thank you, Dinah.

He stuffs his hands in his pockets, casts
a troubled glance at Craig Toomy, and
continues.

                    BOB
          I think I`ve mentioned
          a certain fallacy in
          our thinking. It is
          this: we all assumed,
          when we began to grasp
          the dimensions of this
          Event, that something
          had happened to the <u>rest
          of the world</u>. But the
          evidence doesn`t bear the
          assumption out. What has
          happened has happened to
          us and us alone. I am
          convinced that the world
          as we have always known
          it is ticking along just
          as it always has.
               (a beat, then)
          It`s <u>us</u> -- the passengers
          and ten survivors of
          Flight 29 -- who are
          lost.

Laurel stares at him, trying to stop the shiver running up her spine and failing.

                    LAUREL
          Please tell us what you
          know, Mr. Jenkins. I
          can`t help but feel we`re
          running out of time. And
          fast.

                    BOB
          All right. There`s no
          mess here, but there`s
          a mess on the plane.
          There`s no electricity
          here, but there`s
          electricity on the plane.
          Neither are conclusive,
          of course, but then there
          are the matches. Bethany
          was on the plane, and her
          matches work fine. The
          matches I took from the
          bowl in here wouldn`t
          strike. Mr. Toomy`s
          gun, which he must have
          gotten someplace around
          here, barely fired.
          The carbonated drinks
          are flat. The food is
          tasteless. The air is
          odorless. The same is
          true for sounds. And
          taste and sound are not
          the only off-key elements
          in this place. Take the
          clouds for instance.

                    RUDY
          What about them?

Bob nods out the doorway toward the large
windows looking out on the runway. The low
hanging grey clouds seem to press down on
the horizon outside, squeezing everything
beneath them.

                    BOB
          They haven`t moved since
          we arrived, and I don`t
          think they`re going to
          move. I think the weather
          patterns here have either
          stopped or are running
          down like an old pocket-
          watch.

He pauses for a moment, looking old and
tired.

                    BOB
          And now we come to the
          very hub of the matter.
          I said not fifteen
          minutes ago that it felt
          like lunchtime. It now
          feels much later than
          that to me. Three in the
          afternoon, perhaps four.
          I have a terrible feeling
          that it may start to get
          dark outside before our
          watches tell us it`s
          quarter to ten in the
          morning.

Nick shifts impatiently on his feet.

                    NICK
          Get to it, Mate.

                    BOB
          I think it`s about <u>time</u>,
          not about dimensions, as
          Albert suggested. Suppose
          that~ every now and then,
          a hole appears in the
          time stream. Not a time-
          <u>warp</u>, but a time-<u>rip</u>.
          A rip in the temporal
          fabric.

Gaffney snorts in disbelief.

                    GAFFNEY
          That`s the craziest thing
          I ever heard.

Craig Toomy suddenly seconds him from the
floor below.

                    TOOMY
          Amen!

Bob ignores Toomy, his eyes on Don Gaffney.

                    BOB
          Look around you, Mr.
          Gaffney. What`s happening
          to us -- what we`re <u>in</u> --
          <u>that`s</u> crazy.

Gaffney frowns and sticks his hands deeper

into his pockets.

                    BRIAN
          Go on.

                    BOB
          All right, let us say
          that such rips in the
          fabric of time appear
          every now and then. They
          could be similar to rare
          weather phenomena which
          are sometimes reported:
          upside-down tornadoes,
          circular rainbows,
          daytime starlight.

Brian suddenly mutters to himself.

                    BRIAN
          The Aurora Borealis.

                    BOB
          What?

                    BRIAN
          There was an Aurora
          Borealis over the Mojave
          desert when we left
          L.A.X. We were supposed
          to fly right into it.

                    BOB
          Well, that supports my
          point, doesn`t it. Let us
          say that we did have the
          bad luck to fly into it.

                    BOB (CONT.)
          And that it was a time-
          rip. That means we are no
          longer in our own time,
          ladies and gentlemen.

                    NICK
          Get to the bottom line,
          would you, mate? I agree
          with the lady. It`s
          getting very late in the
          day.

Laurel shoots him a grateful glance as Bob
continues.

                    BOB
          The bottom line? The
          bottom line, I believe,
          is that we have hopped an
          absurdly short distance
          into the past, perhaps
          as little as fifteen
          minutes -- and discovered
          the unlovely truth of
          time-travel: you can`t
          appear in the Texas State
          School Depository on
          November 22, 1963, and
          put a stop to the Kennedy
          assassination; you can`t
          watch the building of
          the pyramids or the
          sack of Rome; you can`t
          investigate the Age of
          the Dinosaurs at first
          hand.

He raises his arms, hands outstretched, as
if to encompass the whole silent world in
which they find themselves.

                    BOB
          Take a good look around
          you, fellow time-
          travelers. This is the
          past. It is empty; it is
          silent. It is a world
          -- perhaps a universe --
          that is clearly unwinding
          around us. Sensory
          input is disappearing.
          Electricity has already
          disappeared. The weather
          is static and fading and
          time itself is winding
          down in a kind of spiral
          that goes faster and
          faster.

                    ALBERT
          Couldn`t this be the
          future?

                    BOB
          I don`t know for sure, of
          course, but this place
          we`re in feels -- I don`t
          know --

Dinah speaks then, drawing their gazes to
her.

                    DINAH
          It feels over.

                         BOB
          Yes. Thank you, dear.
          That`s the word I was
          looking for.

Dinah suddenly lifts her head, cocking an
ear, her body tensing.

                        DINAH
          Mr. Jenkins.

                         BOB
          Yes?

                        DINAH
          The sound I told you
          about before? I can hear
          it again.
                    (a beat, then)
          It`s getting closer.
          Much, much closer.

They all fall silent, their face long and
listening.

Dinah is right.

Now they can all hear it, a low, slowly
gathering roar in the far distance that
sounds suspiciously like SNAP CRACKLE-POP.

And it is getting closer and louder with
every passing second.

Brian is the first to break the silence.

                    BRIAN
          I`m going back out to the
          windows.

He takes off, the others following except
for Laurel and Dinah who sit at a nearby
table.

Nick hesitates, looking at them.

                    NICK
          What about you two?

                    LAUREL
          We can hear it as well as
          we want from here.

                    NICK
          All right, but keep away
          from Mr. Toomy.

Laurel nods as Nick walks out of the
restaurant, following the others.

INT. CENTRAL WAITING ROOM - DAY

The small group, minus Toomy, Laurel, and
Dinah, cluster before one of the huge
windows, looking out on the utterly still
runway.

The day is still dark and overcast, so
dreary it is oppressive.

Nick comes up behind them, staring out the
window.

                    NICK
          What do you make of it,
          Brian?

Brian slowly shakes his head.

                    BRIAN
          All I know is that it`s
          the only sound in town.

                    GAFFNEY
          It`s not in town yet, but
          it`s going to be. And
          soon.

                    BETHANY
          Dinah`s right. We have to
          get out of here. We have
          to get out of here <u>right</u>
          <u>now</u>!

Albert puts his arm around her waist and
she grips his hand in both of hers with
panicky tightness.

                    BRIAN
          Yeah, but where do we
          go? Atlantic City? Miami
          Beach? Club Med?

                    BOB
          You are suggesting,
          Captain Engle, that
          there`s no place we <u>can</u>
          go. I think -- I hope --
          that you`re wrong about
          that. But first, answer

                    BOB (CONT.)
me one question. Can you
refuel the airplane even
if there`s no power?

                    BRIAN
Let`s say that, with the
help of a few able-bodied
men, I could. Then what?

                    BOB
Then we take off again.
That sound - that crunchy
sound -- is coming from
the east. The time-rip
was several thousand
miles west of here. If
we retraced our original
course -- could you do
that?

                    BRIAN
Yes, I could. But why?

                    BOB
Because the rip might
still be there. Don`t you
see? <u>We might be able to
fly back through it</u>!

Nick turns to Brian, rising excitement in
his voice.

                    NICK
He might have something
there, mate. He just
might.

Brian looks back, his face sagging with
hopelessness.

                    BRIAN
          He might or he might not.
          It doesn`t really matter,
          because we`re not going
          anywhere in that plane.

                    RUDY
          Why not? If you could
          refuel it, I don`t see

                    BRIAN
          Remember the matches? The
          ones from the bowl in the
          restaurant? The ones that
          wouldn`t light?

Rudy looks blank, but an expression of
huge dismay dawns on Bob`s face.

He puts his hand to his forehead and takes
a step backward.

Don Gaffney looks at him.

                    GAFFNEY
          What? What does that have
          to do --

                    NICK
          Don`t you see, mate? If
          beer is flat and matches
          won`t light

                    BRIAN
          -- then jet fuel won`t
          burn. It will be as
          used up and worn out as
          everything else in this
          world. I might as well
          fill up the fuel tanks
          with molasses.

That SOUND continues to draw closer and
louder in the distance as they all stare
helplessly at each other, none of them,
not even Bob, saying anything.

PART 2

ACT 1

INT. CLOUD NINE RESTAURANT - DAY

Laurel and Dinah are sitting quietly at their little table when suddenly Dinah turns, looking blindly in Toomy`s direction.

> DINAH
> You mentioned Langoliers
> earlier, Mr. Toomy. What
> are those?

Toomy cranes his neck to look at her, his tone bright and crisp.

> TOOMY
> Ah, the Langoliers. I
> should have known you`d
> be the one to ask about
> them.

Laurel looks at the girl worriedly.

> LAUREL
> Dinah, you shouldn`t talk
> to him --

Toomy shifts his gaze to Laurel.

> TOOMY
> Don`t worry. I wouldn`t
> hurt the child. No more
> than I would have hurt
> that girl. I`m just

                    TOOMY (CONT.)
frightened, that`s all.

                    LAUREL
So am I, but I don`t take
hostages and then try to
shoot teenage boys when
I`m frightened.

Toomy is about to reply, but Dinah breaks
in, her tone as calm as the air outside.

                    DINAH
What about the Langoliers,
Mr. Toomy?

                    TOOMY
Yes, the Langoliers. Well,
I always used to think
they were make-believe.
But now I`m beginning to
wonder - because I hear
it, too. Yes, I do.

                    DINAH
The sound? The sound is
the Langoliers?

                    TOOMY
My father said Langoliers
were little creatures
that lived in closets and
sewers and other dark
places.

                    DINAH
Like elves?

Toomy laughs and shakes his head.

                    TOOMY
          Nothing so pleasant, I`m
          afraid. He said that all
          they really were was hair
          and teeth and fast little
          legs -- their little legs
          were fast, he said, so
          they could catch up with
          bad little boys and girls
          no matter how quickly
          they scampered.

Laurel stiffens.

                    LAUREL
          Stop it. You`re scaring
          the child.

                    DINAH
          No, he`s not. I know
          make-believe when I hear
          it.
               (back to Toomy)
          How many Langoliers did
          he say there were, Mr.
          Toomy?

                    TOOMY
          Thousands, many, many
          thousands. He said there
          had to be, because there
          were <u>millions</u> of bad boys
          and girls scampering
          about the world. My
          father never saw a child

> TOOMY (CONT.)
> run in his entire life.
> They always scampered.
> I think he liked that
> word because it implies
> senseless, directionless,
> non productive motion. But
> the Langoliers -- <u>they</u>
> run. <u>They</u> have purpose.
> In fact, you could say
> that the Langoliers are
> purpose personified.

> DINAH
> What did the kids do that
> was so bad the Langoliers
> had to run after them?

> TOOMY
> You know, I`m glad you
> asked that question.
> Because when my father
> said someone was bad,
> Dinah, what he meant
> was lazy. A lazy person
> couldn`t be part of THE
> BIG PICTURE. No way. And
> he said if you weren`t
> part of THE BIG PICTURE,
> the Langoliers would come
> and take you out of the
> picture completely. He
> said you`d be in your
> bed one night and then
> you`d hear them coming
> -- crunching and smacking
> their way toward you

Laurel suddenly speaks up, her voice flat
and dry, but commanding nonetheless.

                    LAUREL
          <u>That`s enough</u>.

Toomy turns his gaze toward her, his eyes
bright, almost rogueish.

                    TOOMY
          All right. Anything you
          say.

He rolls over on his back and then onto his
other side, away form them. Dinah suddenly
speaks up.

                    DINAH
          I`ll bet you were scared
          of your dad, weren`t you,
          Mr. Toomy?

Toomy looks back over his shoulder at Dinah.
He smiles, but this smile is different
than the others. It is a rueful, hurt
smile with no public relations in it.

                    TOOMY
          <u>You</u> win the cigar, miss.
          I was terrified of him.
          Scared to death, as a
          matter of fact.

                    DINAH
          Was he lying down on the
          job? Did the Langoliers
          finally get him?

Toomy thinks about it for a moment before
replying.

>   TOOMY
>   Yes, I guess he was, and
>   I guess they did.

Dinah stares blindly in his direction for
a moment and then speaks.

>   DINAH
>   Mr. Toomy?

>   TOOMY
>   What?

>   DINAH
>   I`m not the way you see
>   me. I`m not ugly. None of
>   us are.

He looks at her, startled.

>   TOOMY
>   How would you know how
>   you look to me, little
>   blind miss?

>   DINAH
>   You might be surprised.

Laurel looks at the little blind girl, her
disquiet growing.

INT. WAITING ROOM - DAY

The other passengers stand on the far

side of the waiting room, staring out the big windows, and listening to that LOW RATTLING in the far distance and saying nothing. It seems there`s nothing left to say. Don Gaffney breaks the silence.

                    GAFFNEY
          What do we do now?

Brian shrugs helplessly.

                    BRIAN
          I don`t know.

He stares out at his plane, struck by her smooth clean lines and beauty. The Delta 727 sitting to its left looks dowdy by comparison. He can only shake his head in admiration.

                    BRIAN
          God, she looks beautiful,
          doesn`t she?

Nick breaks the mood, looking at Brian.

                    NICK
          How much fuel is left,
          Brian?

                    BRIAN
          When we landed, I had
          less than 600 pounds. To
          get back to where this
          happened, we`d need at
          least fifty thousand.

Bethany takes out a cigarette and sticks one in her mouth, takes out her matches from the plane, and strikes one. It doesn`t light.

                    BETHANY
          Oh-oh.

She strikes the match again -- and again -- and again. Nothing. The others watch.

                    RUDY
          Whatever it is, it seems
          to be catching.

Nick breaks in, his voice tired and depressed.

                    NICK
          I`m going back to the
          restaurant. I don`t like
          leaving our banker friend
          alone with the ladies too
          long.

He takes off across the waiting room for the restaurant.

Brian and the others follow. Albert and Bethany watch.

                    BETHANY
          Come on, let`s go.

They start after the others only to have Albert suddenly stop, yelling at the others.

                    ALBERT
            Wait a minute!

He whirls and hurries back to the window.
He stops, staring out at Flight 29,
noticing what Brian had noticed a few
minutes earlier: the 767 is clean and
smooth and almost impossibly white. It
seems to vibrate in the stillness outside,
especially compared to the 727 sitting to
its left. Bob, Bethany, and the others
cross back toward him.

                    BOB
            Albert? Albert, what`s
            wrong --

Albert suddenly screams as the pieces fall
into place.

                    ALBERT
            <u>Captain Engle</u>! <u>Captain</u>
            <u>Engle, come here</u>! <u>I think</u>
            <u>I have the solution to</u>
            <u>our problem!</u>

EXT. RUNWAY - A FEW MINUTES LATER

Bob and Albert trundle a rolling stairway
toward the American Pride jet as Brian and
Nick tear the emergency slide loose from
the open doorway. Finished they help Bob
and Albert place the stairway with the top
step against the door. Brian runs fleetly
up the stairs, Nick, Bob, and Albert
following. In the distance, to the East,
that CHEW-CRUNCH-WHIR-CHEW continues to

grow closer.

INT. MAIN TERMINAL - DAY

Bethany, Dinah, and Laurel are lined up at the window, staring out at the plane below. Across the waiting room, in the Cloud Nine restaurant, Rudy and Don Gaffney baby-sit Toomy.

                    DINAH
          What are they doing?

                    LAUREL
          They`ve taken the slide
          away and put a stairway
          by the door. Now they`re
          going up.
                    (to Bethany)
          You`re sure you don`t
          know what they`re up to?

Bethany shakes her head.

                    BETHANY
          All I know is Albert
          almost went nuts. He
          said something about the
          plane being more <u>there</u>.
          I didn`t get it. He was
          really jabbering.

                    DINAH
          I just hope they hurry up.
          Because poor Mr. Toomy is
          right. The Langoliers are
          coming.

                    LAUREL
          Dinah, that's just
          something his father made
          up.

Dinah turns her sightless eyes back to
the window, staring eastward where the
CRUNCH-RATTLE-CRUNCH seems to be growing
louder.

                    DINAH
          Maybe once it was make-
          believe, but not anymore.

INT. 727 - FIRST-CLASS CABIN - DAY

The four men come through the open door and
down the alley. They stop at the galley
counter.

                    NICK
          All right, Albert. On
          with the show.

They watch closely as Albert puts down a
book of matches, a bottle of Budweiser,
a can of Pepsi, and a peanut-butter-and
jelly sandwich from the restaurant cold-
case. Albert takes a deep breath.

                    ALBERT
          Okay, let's see what we
          got here.

INT. WAITING ROOM - DAY INTO DUSK

Don Gaffney leaves the restaurant and joins the women before the windows.

                    GAFFNEY
          It looks different
          outside.

Dinah stares blindly at the window, her face an imprint of loneliness and fear.

                    DINAH
          The light`s going. That`s
          what`s different.

They gaze out the window.

Dinah is right.

The day has visibly darkened. Laurel glances at Don.

                    LAUREL
          How`s Mr. Toomy?

Gaffney laughs without much humor.

                    GAFFNEY
          You won`t believe it.
          He`s gone to sleep.

INT. CLOUD NINE RESTAURANT - DUSK INTO NIGHT

Craig Toomy lays unmoving on the floor as Rudy rises from a table, walks over to him, and bends down.

> **RUDY**
> Hey. Hey, you awake?

Nothing from Toomy, not even the flicker of an eyelid. Rudy pokes him in the side. Still nothing. He straightens, steps over him, and goes to the velvet ropes to watch the others. Behind him Toomy cracks an eyelid, stares at him for a moment, and then begins to work at loosening the rope that binds his hands.

INT. 727 - FIRST CLASS GALLEY -DUSK INTO NIGHT

Albert picks up the book of matches and holds them aloft for the others to see.

> **ALBERT**
> Exhibit A. The book
> of matches from the
> restaurant.

Albert tears a match from the book and strikes it. It doesn`t light. He keeps trying, but the match still won`t light. Brian shrugs hopelessly.

> **BRIAN**
> I guess that does it.
> There`s nothing

Nick sniffs the air and suddenly bursts in.

                    NICK
          I smelled it! I smelled
          the sulphur! Try another
          one, Albert.

Instead, Albert strikes the same match a
third time -- and this time it flares and
lights. But it does not just gutter out;
rather it flares brightly and begins to
burn the paper stick. The teenager looks
up at the others, a wild grin on his face.

                   ALBERT
          You see? You see?

He shakes the match out, and pulls another.
This one lights on the first strike. He
bends the cover of the match books back
and touches the lit flame to the other
matches, just as Bob had done earlier in
the restaurant.

Only this time, they all flare brightly
alight.

Albert looks at the others eagerly.

                   ALBERT
          You see what it means? We
          brought our own time with
          us! That`s the past out
          there -- and everywhere,
          I guess, east of the hole
          we came through - but the
          present is still in here.
          Still caught inside this
          airplane!

                    BOB
          Bravo, Albert! The beer!
          Try the beer!

Albert spins the cap off the beer while
Nick fishes an unbroken glass from the
drinks trolley. The teenager sniffs the
top of the open bottle and then tips it
toward Brian.

                  ALBERT
          Smell.

Brian does and begins to grin.

                   BRIAN
          By God, it sure <u>smells</u>
          like beer.

Nick holds out the glass he got.

                   NICK
          Pour it. Hurry up, mate
          -- my sawbones says
          suspense is bad for the
          old ticker.

Albert pours the beer and their smiles
fade. The beer is flat. Utterly flat. It
simply sits in the whiskey glass Nick had
found, looking like an old urine sample.

INT. WAITING ROOM - DUSK INTO NIGHT

Rudy walks across the waiting room toward
the small group at the window. The shadows
seem to lengthen as he walks, <u>the light</u>

<u>outside doing a visible swan dive into darkness</u>.

                    RUDY
          Christ almighty, it`s
          getting dark!

They look around as Rudy joins them.

                  GAFFNEY
          You`re supposed to be
          watching the nut.

                    RUDY
          Don`t worry. He`s still
          out.

He cocks an ear, listening hard.

                    RUDY
          Damn, is that sound
          <u>creepy</u>? It`s like a bunch
          of coked-up termites in a
          balsa-wood glider.

Dinah looks up at Laurel.

                  DINAH
          I think we better check
          on Mr. Toomy. I`m worried
          about him.

                  LAUREL
          If he`s unconscious,
          Dinah, there isn`t
          anything we can do --

> DINAH
> I don`t think he`s
> unconscious. I don`t
> think he`s even asleep.

> LAUREL
> All right, let`s have a
> look.

She takes the little girl`s hand and they start back for the restaurant.

INT. CLOUD NINE RESTAURANT - NIGHT

Craig Toomy continues to work his hands against the knotted rope, finally pulling one free. He uses it to free his other one and quickly gets to his feet. He notices the two women walking back toward the restaurant, and slips behind the counter, finds a butcher knife, and crouches behind the cash register, watching Laurel and Dinah approach. He grips the knife firmly and waits.

INT. 727 -FIRST-CLASS GALLEY - NIGHT

Nick, confused and dispirited, looks from Albert to Bob.

> NICK
> So the matches work, but
> the lager doesn`t. What
> does that mean

All at once a small mushroom cloud of bubbles burst from nowhere in the bottom

of the glass. They rise rapidly, spread,
and burst in a thin head at the top. Nick
and the other`s eyes widen.

                    BOB
          Apparently it takes a
          moment or two for things
          to catch up.

He takes the glass, drinks, and smacks his
lips.

                    BOB
          Excellent. I can say
          without doubt it`s the
          best glass of beer I ever
          drank in my life.

Albert pours more beer into the glass. This
time it comes out foaming. The head over
spills the rim and runs down the outside.
Brian picks the glass up and drinks, then
laughs out loud.

                    BRIAN
          You`re right. It`s the
          best goddamn beer there
          ever was. Try the Pepsi,
          Albert.

Albert opens the can and they all hear
the familiar pop-hisss of carbonation. He
takes a deep drink and when he lowers the
can, he is grinning -- but there are tears
in his eyes when he speaks in the plummy
tones of a head waiter.

                    ALBERT
          Gentlemen, the Pepsi-Cola
          is very good today.

They all begin to laugh.

INT. NINE - CLOUD RESTAURANT - NIGHT

Don Gaffney catches up with Laurel and
Dinah just as they enter the restaurant.

                    GAFFNEY
          I thought I`d better

He stops, looking around, realizing Craig
Toomy is no longer there.

                    GAFFNEY
          Oh, my God. Where is he?

                    LAUREL
          I don`t

                    DINAH
          Be quiet.

Her head turns slowly, like the lamp of a
dead searchlight.

For a moment there is no sound in the
restaurant. Dinah suddenly stops and
points toward the cash register.

                    DINAH
          There. He`s hiding over
          there. Behind something.

                    GAFFNEY
          How do you know that? I
          don`t hear --

                    DINAH
          I do. I hear his heart.
          It`s beating very fast
          and very hard. He`s
          scared to death. I feel
          so sorry for him.

She suddenly lets Laurel`s hand go and
steps forward. Laurel yells.

                    LAUREL
          Dinah, no!

Dinah takes no notice. She walks toward the
cash register, arms out, fingers seeking
possible obstacles.

                    DINAH
          Mr. Toomy? Please, come
          out. We don`t want to
          hurt you. Please don`t be
          afraid --

Craig Toomy suddenly rises from behind the
cash register, eyes blazing with insanity,
butcher knife raised. He shrieks and rushes
at her.

                    TOOMY
          Youuuuuuuuuuuuuuuu

Don Gaffney shoves Laurel out of the way,
diving to intercept toomy, but he`s too

late. Toomy reaches the little girl, buries the butcher knife in her chest without stopping, and runs past Laurel and Gaffney into the terminal, still shrieking.

Dinah stands there for a moment, her hands fluttering over the wooden handle of the knife jutting out the front of her dress, exploring it.

Then she sinks slowly, gracefully, to the floor.

INT. 727 -FIRST-CLASS GALLEY - NIGHT

Albert, Nick, Brian, and Bob pass the peanut-butter-and-jelly sandwich around, each taking a bite. Nick finishes it off with a satisfied smile.

                    NICK
          You`re a genius, Albert.
          You know that, don`t you?
          Nothing but pure genius.

Albert flushes happily.

                    ALBERT
          It wasn`t much. I saw
          what was happening with
          Bethany`s matches and
          thought --

Bethany suddenly appears on the ladder in the open doorway only a few feet away, screaming at them.

                         BETHANY
              Come! You`ve got to come!

She is panting, out of breath, and reels
backward on the platform of the ladder,
almost falling. Nick leaps forward,
cupping his hand on the nape of her neck,
and pulling her into the plane. Bethany
hardly seems to notice as she keeps on
talking.

                         BETHANY
              Please come! He`s stabbed
              her. I think she`s dying.

                          NICK
              Who has stabbed whom? Who
              is dying?

                         BETHANY
              That blind girl. Dinah.
              Mr. Toomy did it.

                          NICK
              Bloody hell! Albert, you
              come with me. Brian, keep
              the plane here till we
              get Dinah aboard. Bob,
              bottom of the stairs.
              Keep an eye out for
              Toomy.

With that he and Albert dive down the
ladder, leaving Brian, Bob, and Bethany
staring after them.

INT. CLOUD NINE RESTAURANT - NIGHT

Laurel kneels over Dinah. Don Gaffney and Rudy stand behind her, looking down anxiously. The little girl looks up at Laurel, speaking in a fading whisper.

>   DINAH
>   Get -get out of here --

A curdle of blood escapes her mouth and runs down her cheek. Laurel brushes damp hair from her forehead.

>   LAUREL
>   Don`t try to talk, Dinah
>   --

Nick hurries into the restaurant, followed by Albert. He pushes past Rudy and Gaffney and kneels next to Dinah.

He speaks cheerily, but his eyes have darkened.

>   NICK
>   Hello, love. I see you`ve
>   been air conditioned. Not
>   to worry; you`ll be right
>   as rain in no time flat.

Nick moves her head, very gently, until her cheek is about resting on the carpet.

>   NICK
>   Hurt?

                    DINAH
          Yes. Hot. Hurts to --
          breathe.

From outside comes the HIGH SCREAM of
airplane engines firing.

Don, Rudy, Laurel, and Albert all glance
in the direction of the windows. Nick,
however, never looks away from the girl.

                    NICK
          Do you feel like coughing,
          Dinah?

                    DINAH
          Yes -- no -- I don`t
          know.

                    NICK
          It`s better if you don`t.
          If you get that tickly
          feeling, try to ignore
          it. And don`t talk
          anymore, right?

She whispers, her words suddenly having
great urgency.

                    DINAH
          Don`t -- hurt -- Mr.
          Toomy.

                    NICK
          No, love. Wouldn`t think
          of it.

                    DINAH
          -- don`t trust -- you.

Nick leans down, kisses her cheek, and
whispers in her ear.

                    NICK
          But you can, you know
          -- trust me, I mean. For
          now, all you`ve got to do
          is lie there and let me
          take care of things.

He raises back on his knee, looking at
Rudy.

                    NICK
          Mr. Warwick, bring me
          half a dozen tablecloths
          from that grotty little
          pub around the corner,
          would you?

Rudy takes off. Nick looks at Laurel.

                    NICK
          Does the sight of blood
          bother you?

                    LAUREL
          I can deal with it if I
          have to.

                    NICK
          Good. You`re my nurse
          then.

He looks down at Dinah with a smile.

                    NICK

      Give me a minute or two, Dinah, and
        we`ll get that knife out of you.
Dinah glances up at him, suddenly speaking.

                    DINAH
            They`re closer. You
            really, really have to
            hurry.

More blood bubbles out of her mouth. Don
Gaffney turns away. Nick`s cheery smile
doesn`t change a bit.

                    NICK
            I know.

INT. LOWER LOBBY - NIGHT

Craig Toomy comes down the metal steps of
the frozen escalator into the lower lobby.

He stops there, staring around him, dazed,
that CHEW-CRUNCH CHEW SOUND growing closer
in the distance. His eyes fasten on a
door tucked between the Avis Desk and the
Bangor Travel Agency. It reads AIRPORT
SERVICES. He dives for it, disappearing
inside.

INT. AIRPORT SERVICES OFFICE - NIGHT 122

Toomy moves through the almost total

darkness, the chewing sound of the Langoliers muffled now. He finds a desk and sits, his hands feeling around. He almost immediately finds a letter opener and sets it in front of him. His father`s voice echoes inside his head again.

                    ROGER TOOMY (V.O.)
          That`s right, Craiggy-
          weggy. You just sit here
          in the dark. When the
          time comes to move --
          I`ll tell you.

Craig grins and nods, speaking out loud.

                    TOOMY
          All right, father.
          Anything you say.

His fingers find a sheet of paper and spider to the right hand corner. He tears smoothly downward. <u>Riii-ip</u> goes the paper and Toomy smiles, beginning to relax at last.

ACT 2

INT. CLOUD NINE RESTAURANT - NIGHT

Nick finishes his examination of Dinah and rises to his feet, looking at Albert and Don Gaffney.

> NICK
> We`ll need a litter to
> take her on board the
> plane. You and Mr. Gaffney
> are designated litter-
> finders. Mr. Gaffney,
> check behind the counter.
> I expect you`ll find some
> sharp knives there.

Don Gaffney goes behind the counter without a word and begins searching. Rudy returns from the Red Baron Bar with an arm load of red-and-white checked tablecloths. Nick takes them. His eyes swing back to Albert. The teenager`s face is now only a circle of white above the deeper shadows of Dinah`s body. The darkness of night has almost arrived.

> NICK
> Remember, your mission
> isn`t to recapture Mr.
> Toomy. Your job is to get
> a stretcher and bring it
> here as quick as you can.

Gaffney returns with a pair of butcher

knives and offers Albert one, but the teenager shakes his head and looks at Rudy instead.

                    ALBERT
          Could I have one of those
          tablecloths, please?

Don Gaffney looks at him like he`s crazy.

                    GAFFNEY
          A tablecloth? What in
          God`s name for?

                    ALBERT
          I`ll show you.

Albert goes behind the counter, and picks up an old-fashioned two-slice toaster sitting well back on the counter. He jerks the plug out of the wall socket and returns to the others.

He takes one of the tablecloths, spreads it, and places the toaster in one corner. He turns it over twice, wrapping the toaster like a Christmas present. Then he grabs the loose end of the tablecloth and stands. The wrapped toaster has become a rock in a makeshift sling. He smiles at the others apologetically.

                    ALBERT
          When I was a kid, we used
          to play Indiana Jones. I
          made something like this
          -- an old sash weight

                    ALBERT (CONT.)
          in a blanket -- and
          pretended it was my whip.
          I almost broke my brother
          David`s arm with it.

Nick looks at Albert`s makeshift weapon
dubiously, but only nods.

                      NICK
          Good enough, then. Now
          go find a stretcher and
          bring it back. If you
          don`t find anything in
          ten minutes just come
          back and we`ll carry her.

Laurel looks at Nick worriedly.

                     LAUREL
          You can`t do that. If
          there`s internal bleeding
          --

Nick cuts her off.

                      NICK
          There`s internal bleeding
          already. And ten minutes
          is all the time I think
          we can spare.

Laurel opens her mouth to argue, but
Dinah`s husky whisper stops her.

                     DINAH
          Laurel, he`s right.

Gaffney slips the knife into his belt, looking at Albert.

                    GAFFNEY
          Come on, son.

They exit the restaurant, cutting across the terminal toward the dead escalator. Nick falls back to his knees beside the blind little girl.

                    NICK
          How are you feeling,
          Dinah?

Dinah replies faintly.

                    DINAH
          Hurts bad.

                    NICK
          Yes, of course it does.
          The knife is in your
          lung, and it`s got to
          come out. You know that,
          don`t you?

Dinah looks up at him with her dark, unseeing eyes.

                    DINAH
          Yes. Scared.

                    NICK
          So am I, Dinah. So am I.

Dinah makes a reply none of them can hear.

Nick swallows, arms sweat off his forehead
in a quick gesture, and turns to Laurel.

> NICK
>> Fold two of those
>> tablecloths into square
>> pads. Thick as you can.
>> Kneel beside me. Close
>> as you can get. Warwick,
>> take off your belt.

Both comply at once. Nick looks at Laurel
on the other side of Dinah.

> NICK
>> I`m going to grasp the
>> handle of the knife and
>> draw it out. The moment
>> it`s out, place one of
>> your pads over the wound
>> and press. Press <u>hard</u>. Do
>> you understand?

Laurel nods. Dinah mutters something
indistinct. Nick draws in a long breath
and then lets it out.

> NICK
>> Jesus help me.

He wraps his slim, long-fingered hands
around the handle of the knife and pulls.
Dinah shrieks. A great gout of blood spews
from her mouth, splattering Laurel who is
leaning forward. She recoils. Nick barks
at her without looking around.

                    NICK
          No! Don`t you dare go
          weak-sister on me! Don`t
          you <u>dare</u>!

Laurel leans forward, gagging and
shuddering. The blade emerges from Dinah`s
chest, glimmering in the fading light. The
little blind girl`s chest heaves and there
is a high, unearthly whistling sound as
the wound sucks inward. Nick yells.

                    NICK
          <u>Now</u>! Press down! As hard
          as you can!

Laurel does as told, pressing the table
cloth against the girl`s chest with all
her might, she and Nick working madly to
save Dinah`s life.

INT. LOWER LOBBY - NIGHT

Don Gaffney and Albert reach the bottom of
the dead escalator, looking around in the
darkness. Albert`s eyes fasten on the door
Craig Toomy went through a few minutes
before. He nods at it.

                    ALBERT
          Let`s try in there.

They start toward the door to AIRPORT
SERVICES, Don Gaffney leading the way.

INT. AIRPORT SERVICES OFFICE - NIGHT

Toomy looks up in the darkness, listening to the voices approach the other side of the door.

                    GAFFNEY`S (O.S.)
          Do you think it`s locked?

                    ALBERT (O.S.)
          Well, there`s only one
          way to find out.

Toomy grasps the letter opener in his hand, rises from the desk, and slips behind the door just as it opens. Don Gaffney steps into the gloom, He flicks his Zippo lighter and a low flame appears, illuminating the office in flickering shadows. Gaffney steps further into the room, holding the lighter up.

                    GAFFNEY
          Hey, kid! Albert! Look!

He points at the back wall where a white plastic box with a red cross on it is mounted. Leaning below it is a folded stretcher. Albert steps further into the room, but his eyes aren`t fixed on the stretcher. Oh, no. He is staring at the desk in the center of the room. On it are a heaped tangle of paper strips.

                    ALBERT
          Look out! Look out, he`s
          in h --

                    TOOMY
          You`re one of them, too,
          aren`t you? A Langolier.
          Well, screw you. I`m
          going to Boston and you
          can`t stop me. <u>None</u> of
          you can stop me.

Craig Toomy steps out from behind the door and strikes before Albert can finish. He buries the letter opener fist-deep in Gaffney`s neck. Don screams and drops the lighter. It strikes the floor and gutters sickishly. Albert shouts in surprise as he sees Toomy grab the letter-opener buried in Gaffney`s neck and jerk it free. Gaffney screams again, louder this time, and goes sprawling backward over the desk. The strips of paper go flying. Toomy turns toward Albert, flicking a spray of bloody droplets from the letter-opener. He grins at Albert. Albert backs for the door, Toomy following him, letter-opener raised high.

INT. LOWER LOBBY - NIGHT

Albert comes through the door, Toomy gliding after him like a shadow dancing in the dark.

Albert tries to get hold of his panic, just barely succeeds, and begins to whirl the toaster around above his head. Toomy moves in, weaving the top half of his body side to side like a snake coming out of a basket. His father speaks to him inside his head.

                    ROGER TOOMY (V.O.)
              That`s right, Craiggy-
              weggy. If you have to
              pick them off one by one,
              do it. Do it and get to
              Boston!

Toomy stops, looking sorrowfully at
the white-faced Albert in the darkness
opposite him.

                         TOOMY
              I`m sorry. I`m really,
              really sorry, but I have
              to do this. If you were
              in my position, you`d
              understand.

He continues to advance on Albert, Albert
backing away toward the United Airlines
ticket desk. He begins to pendulum the
toaster more rapidly, his sweaty hands
clutching the twist of tablecloth. Craig
Toomy suddenly shrieks.

                         TOOMY
              I`m going to Boston! I`m
              going to --

Toomy darts forward, letter-opener in hand
just as Albert brings the toaster around
with a hard snap of his wrists. It catches
Toomy in the shoulder, spinning him back
against a wall. He slams into it, almost
falling, rights himself, and stands there,
breathing hard, staring at Albert with cold
glittery eyes. Then he starts toward the

young man again, letter-opener in hand.
Albert is terrified of what he has done,
but is even more terrified of Toomy. Toomy
stabs at him and he sidesteps and swings
the tablecloth sidearm. It connects with
Toomy`s forehead, and the man goes flying
backward. He hits the floor, slamming
his head with a sickening thud, and lays
there, suddenly silent.

Albert stands there, sobbing for breath,
the weighted tablecloth dangling from his
hand. Then he takes two shambling steps
toward the escalator, bows deeply, and
vomits on the floor.

INT. CLOUD NINE RESTAURANT - NIGHT

Rudy stands above Nick and Laurel, the two
of them bent over Dinah, working on her.
But Rudy isn`t paying any attention. He`s
listening to the sounds of the struggle on
the level below. Nick gets the second pad
of tablecloth under Dinah and lifts her up
off the floor. He grunts urgently at Rudy.

                    NICK
          Belt.

Rudy doesn`t move, his attention on the
noise below.

                    RUDY
          Do you hear that? Do you
          think Toomy got them --

Nick kicks backward like a mule, connecting

with Rudy`s shin.

                    RUDY
          Ow!

                    NICK
          Belt! Now!

Rudy drops clumsily to one knee and slips
his belt under the pad around Dinah`s
back. He pants and sweat rolls down his
face in wide streams as he fumbles to do
as told. Nick barks at him.

                    NICK
          Quick. I can`t hold her
          up forever!

Rudy gets the belt underneath the pad. Nick
lowers Dinah, reaches across the girl`s
small body, and lifts her left shoulder
long enough to pull the belt out the other
side. He loops it over her chest, and
cinches it tight. He puts the belt`s free
end in Laurel`s free hand and stands up.

                    NICK
          Keep the pressure on. I`m
          going downstairs.

Laurel grabs the belt and looks up at him.
Worry floods her face.

                    LAUREL
          Be careful. Please, be
          careful.

Nick grins down at her in the gathering gloom.

>   NICK
>   Of course. It`s how I get
>   along.

His hand reaches down and gives her shoulder a warm squeeze.

>   NICK
>   You did very well,
>   Laurel. Thank you.

She flashes him a smile and he begins to turn away when a small hand gropes out and catches the cuff of his blue-jeans. He looks down to see that Dinah`s blind eyes are open again.

>   DINAH
>   Don`t --

A choked sneezing fit shakes her. Blood flies from her nose in a spray of fine mist. She goes on anyway, her blind eyes on Nick.

>   DINAH
>   Don`t -- you -- kill him!

Nick stops, looking at her thoughtfully.

>   NICK
>   Why not? The bugger
>   stabbed you, you know.

Her narrow chest strains against the belt.
The bloodstained tablecloth pad heaves.
She manages to whisper one thing more.

                    DINAH
          All -- I know -- is
          that we need him.

Her eyes close again and Nick goes to turn
when Laurel speaks.

                    LAUREL
          I`d do as she asks,
          Nick. She`s something --
          special.

Nick looks at her a moment, then nods, and
hurries toward the main lobby and the dead
escalator.

INT. 767 - COCKPIT - NIGHT

Brian takes a seat and crosses himself as
he thumbs back the black plastic shield
that covers the screen of the INS video
display terminal, half expecting it to be
smooth and black. Instead it reads "LAST
PROGRAM COMPLETE" in cool blue-green and
beneath that, "NEW PROGRAM? Y/N." Brian
types in "Y", then: "REVERSE AP 29: LAX/
LOGAN." Numbers begin to flash on the
screen. Brian sits back, watching them.
Bethany appears in the doorway behind him.

                    BETHANY
          Captain Engle, why aren`t
          they back yet?

Brian replies without turning from his computer.

                    BRIAN
        I can`t say.

                    BETHANY
        I asked Bob -- Mr.
        Jenkins -- if he could
        see anyone moving inside
        the terminal, and he said
        he couldn`t. What if
        they`re all dead?

                    BRIAN
        I`m sure they`re not. But
        if it will make you feel
        better, why don`t you
        join him at the bottom of
        the ladder.

She stares at his turned back as he continues to work on the computer.

                    BETHANY
        Are you scared?

                    BRIAN
        Yes. I sure am.

She smiles a little.

                    BETHANY
        I`m sort of glad. It`s
        bad to be scared all be
        yourself.

She leaves as Brian watches "PROGRAM COMPLETE" flash up on his monitor. A second later it is followed by "THANK YOU FOR FLYING AMERICAN PRIDE." He sits back, murmuring to himself.

                    BRIAN
          You`re welcome, I`m sure.

EXT. 767 - NIGHT

Bob hears footsteps on the ladder behind him and turns quickly. It is only Bethany, descending slowly and carefully. The CRUNCH-CHEW-CRUNCH SOUND coming out of the east is growing louder. He smiles at the girl as she joins him.

                    BOB
          Hi, Bethany. May I
          borrow another of your
          cigarettes?

She offers the depleted pack to him, then takes one herself. She lights them easily with a match, looking anxiously toward the terminal.

                    BETHANY
          Any sign of them?

                    BOB
          Well, it all depends on
          what you mean by "any
          sign." I think I heard
          some shouting before you
          came down.

Bethany nods, anxiously puffing on her cigarette.

                    BETHANY
          I hope Dinah`s going to
          be all right, but I don`t
          know. He cut her really
          bad.

                    BOB
          Did you see the Captain?

Bethany nods.

                    BETHANY
          He`s programming his
          instruments, or something.

Jenkins draws on his cigarette, the glowing ember momentarily illuminating a pair of tired, terrified eyes. He slowly shakes his head.

                    BOB
          Dear girl, I hope we
          never have to find out.

INT. LOWER LOBBY - NIGHT

Nick comes down the dead escalator, pausing at the bottom as he picks out a huddled figure in the darkness. The figure suddenly speaks and he realizes it`s Albert.

                    ALBERT
          Don`t step in my puke.

Nick walks over to the bent over boy,
putting his arm around him. Albert slowly
straightens.

Nick speaks to him quietly.

                    NICK
          Where are they, Albert?
          Gaffney and Toomy?

Albert points to a crumpled shape on the
flood.

                    ALBERT
          Mr. Toomy`s there. Mr.
          Gaffney`s in the Airport
          Services office. Mr. Toomy
          was in there. Behind the
          door, I guess. He killed
          Mr. Gaffney because Mr.
          Gaffney walked in first.
          If I`d walked in first,
          he would have killed me
          instead.

Albert swallows hard. His voice has begun
to quake.

                    ALBERT
          Then I killed Mr. Toomy.
          I had to. He came after
          me, see? He found another
          knife someplace and he
          came after me.

Nick looks at him patiently.

                    NICK
          Can you get hold of
          yourself, Albert?

                    ALBERT
          I don`t know. I never
          k-k-killed anyone before,
          and

Albert chokes up, uttering a strangled,
miserable sob.

                    NICK
          I know. It`s a horrible
          thing, but it can be
          gotten over. I know. And
          you must get over it,
          Albert. Now. The sound is
          louder.

He lifts his head, nodding toward the east
where the CRUNCH CHEW-CRUNCH is approaching
from. He leaves Albert to listen to it as
he goes to Toomy and kneels by his side.
The man is still alive, breathing with a
harsh rasp. But it is his face that grabs
Nick`s attention. There is a deep dent in
his forehead, pouring blood. Nick shakes
his head with a soft whistle.

                    NICK
          He did this with a
          toaster? Jesus and Mary,
          Tom, Dick, and Harry.

He rises, looking at Albert who is bent
over again, breathing hard.

                    NICK
          He`s not dead.

Albert straightens slowly, looking at him
amazed.

                    ALBERT
          He`s not?

                    NICK
          Listen to him yourself.
          Out for the count, but
          still in the game. Let`s
          check on Mr. Gaffney --
          maybe he got off lucky,
          too. And what about the
          stretcher?

                    ALBERT
          Huh?

Albert looks at him dumbly. Nick repeats
himself patiently as they walk toward the
Airport Services door.

                    NICK
          The stretcher?

                    ALBERT
          Oh. We found it.

                    NICK
          You did? Super!

Albert stops just outside the door, squats
and feels around. He stands up with Don
Gaffney`s Zippo lighter in his hand.

                    ALBERT
          Mr. Gaffney`s on the
          other side of the desk, I
          think.

He sparks the lighter to life and steps
through the door, Nick following.

INT. AIRPORT SERVICES OFFICE - NIGHT

They step into the office and stop. Don
Gaffney lies face up on the desk, unseeing
eyes open, a look of terrible surprise
on his face. He hadn`t gotten off lucky
after all. Nick goes to the wall, pulls
down the collapsible stretcher, and turns
to Albert. The young man stands there,
staring at Gaffney`s body in dazed horror.

                    NICK
          Keep it together, Albert.
          That`s all there is to
          it -- just keep things
          together and you`ll be
          fine.

He turns and disappears out the door,
carrying the stretcher. Albert follows
just as the lighter gutters out, enclosing
the room in darkness again.

INT. LOWER LOBBY - NIGHT

They cross the lobby, Nick stopping by
Toomy. He hands the stretcher to Albert
and claps him on the shoulder.

                    NICK
          Take the stretcher
          upstairs. I`ll join you
          directly.

                    ALBERT
          What you going are to do?

                    NICK
          I want to see if there`s
          anything else we can use
          in the office.

Albert looks at him in the darkness, hardly
able to make out his face.

                    ALBERT
          I don`t believe you.

Nick smiles, replying in an oddly gentle
voice.

                    NICK
          Nor do you have to. Go
          on, Albert. I`ll join
          you soon. And don`t look
          back.

Albert stares at him a moment longer,
then turns and trudges toward the frozen
escalator, his head down, the stretcher
dangling like a suitcase from his right
hand. He doesn`t look back. Nick kneels
beside Craig Toomy. He is still out, but
his breathing seems a little more regular.
Nick reaches out, putting a hand over
Toomy`s mouth and nose. He hesitates a

moment, then.

> NICK
> Better than the bastard
> deserves.

He clamps down with his hand, closing off his mouth and nose. The sound of Toomy`s harsh breathing suddenly stops, the lobby deadeningly silent. Then Dinah`s words tumble through Nick`s mind.

> DINAH (V.O.)
> Don`t you kill him!
> We need him! Do you
> understand me? We need
> him!

Nick suddenly releases the unconscious man, Toomy`s harsh breathing rattling through the lobby again. He squats there, looking at Toomy thoughtfully when Rudy suddenly speaks from the head of the escalator.

> RUDY
> Mr. Hopewell? Nick? Are
> you coming?

Nick snaps out of it and lifts his head, calling back.

> NICK
> In a jiffy!

He reaches out for Toomy`s face again, his hand prepared to cut off his breathing and snuff out his life, only to hesitate, staring at him. Then he abruptly rises, heading for the escalator.

ACT 3

EXT. RUNWAY -767 - NIGHT

Bethany, bored, throws the tail end of her
butt away, and starts up the ladder to the
plane when Bob cries out.

> BOB
> I think they`re coming
> out!

She turns and runs back down the ladder,
looking toward the terminal. A series of
dark blobs are emerging from the luggage
bay and crawling along the conveyor belt.
Bob and Bethany run to meet them on the
tarmac. Dinah is strapped to the stretcher,
Rudy at one end, Nick at the other. Rudy is
already breathing hard. Albert and Laurel
follow behind.

> BETHANY
> Let me help.

Rudy gives up his end of the stretcher
willingly.

> NICK
> Try not to jiggle her.
> Albert, get on Bethany`s
> end and help us take her
> up the stairs.

Bethany looks at Albert as he lends her a
hand.

                    BETHANY
          How bad is she?

                    ALBERT
          Unconscious, but still
          alive.

Bob walks alongside Nick, raising his voice
to be heard over the wounded-transmission
noise that is quickly becoming the dominant,
maddening voice within the CRUNCH-CHEW-
CRUNCH sound.

                     BOB
          Where are the others?

                    NICK
          Gaffney`s dead and Toomy
          might as well be.

He stops at the foot of the stairs, glancing
back at Albert and Bethany.

                    NICK
          Mind you keep your end
          up, you two.

They move the stretcher slowly and
carefully up the stairs, Nick walking
backward and bent over the forward end,
Albert and Bethany holding the stretcher
up at forehead level.

INT. 767 - NIGHT

Brian steps out of the cockpit as Nick,
Albert, and Bethany lay the stretcher

across the center aisle, snugging it down
with seat belts. Brian leans over the
seats, staring at Dinah and her blood-
soaked compresses.

Her face is very pale, her breathing
shallow and slow. Brian looks at Nick as
the Brit works to secure the stretcher.

> BRIAN
> It`s bad, isn`t it?

> NICK
> Bad enough.

> BRIAN
> Will she live until we
> get back?

Nick suddenly snaps, shouting at him.

> NICK
> How in the hell should I
> know? I`m a soldier, not
> a bloody sawbones.

The others freeze, looking at him with
cautious eyes. Nick lowers his gaze with
a mutter.

> NICK
> Sorry. Time travel plays
> the very devil with one`s
> nerves, doesn`t it?

Laurel reaches out, touching his arm.

                    LAUREL
          No need to apologize.
          We`re all under strain.

Nick smiles tiredly and touches her hair.

                    NICK
          You`re a sweetheart,
          Laurel, and no mistake.

Brian lifts his head, listening to the
approaching CRUNCH CHEW-CRUNCH-WHIR sound.

It seems to be growing ever louder and
closer. He looks at the others.

                    BRIAN
          I`m going to start the
          other engine now and pull
          as close as I can get to
          that 727.

He points out the open door at the Delta
plane.

It`s just a grey lump in the darkness
outside.

                    BRIAN
          While I do that, the four
          of you bring over the
          hose cart -- there`s one
          sitting by the other jet
          way. Got it?

They all nod. He continues.

                    BRIAN
          Go to it, then. Bethany?
          Mr. Warwick? Go down with
          them. Pull the ladder
          away from the plane,
          and when I`ve got it
          repositioned, place it
          next to the overlapping
          wings.

They nod again and dive for the door as
Brian turns back for the cockpit.

EXT. 767 - TARMAC - NIGHT INTO DAY

They all pile down the ladder, Bethany and
Rudy pulling it back as the others hurry
across the tarmac. Laurel suddenly stops,
pointing at the hose cart.

                    LAUREL
          My God, look!

The others stop with her, staring at the
hose cart. They can see it again! Laurel
glances up at the sky. <u>Its inky blackness
is turning to the cold slate grey of dawn
before their very eyes</u>.

                    LAUREL
          It`s coming daylight
          again already. How long
          has it been since it got
          dark?

Bob glances at his watch.

                    BOB
          Less than forty minutes.

                    NICK
          Well, come on. We can`t
          worry about it now.

They all start toward the hose cart again.
Laurel glances at Nick as they walk.

                    LAUREL
          What`s going to happen to
          Mr. Toomy?

                    NICK
          I don`t know. All I know
          is when the chips were
          down, I did what Dinah
          and you wanted. I left
          him lying unconscious on
          the floor.

She flashes him a grateful smile as they
come to a halt by the cart. It is a small
vehicle with a tank on the back, an open-
air cab, and thick black hoses coiled on
either side.

Nick turns to Laurel, putting an arm around
her waist to lift her up. He smiles and
gives her waist a brief squeeze.

                    NICK
          Would you like to go to
          dinner with me when and
          if we make it back to
          L.A.?

She smiles back hesitantly.

> LAUREL
> Yes. That would be
> something to look forward
> to.

> NICK
> For me, too.

Nick lifts Laurel up and into the cab. She looks back as the three men line themselves up along the rear of the cart, Nick in the middle. He yells at the other two above the scream of the 747.

> NICK
> All right, then -- all
> together!

They push and Laurel pulls the wheel with all her might to the right. The yellow cart describes a small circle on the grey tarmac and begins to roll toward the 767, which is trundling slowly into position on the left hand side of the parked Delta jet. The plane comes to a halt and the turbines die, leaving only the steady low rumble of the APUs -- Brian is now running all four of them. They are not, however, loud enough to cover the growing CHEW-CRUNCH-CHEW sound from the east. As it draws closer, it is fragmenting, changing from one uniform sound to sounds within sounds. And the sum total is beginning to sound <u>horrible</u>, like animals at feeding time, sent through an amplifier and blown up to grotesque proportions! The foursome pushing the hose cart have to shout to make themselves heard over it.

                    BOB
          Maybe if we could see it,
          we could deal with it.

Albert throws him a dubious glance.

                  ALBERT
          I don`t think so.

EXT. PLANE - DAY

Brian appears in the door of the stopped 767 and steps onto the platform. He points to the overlapping wings. As Rudy and Bethany roll him in that direction, he listens to the approaching noise. CHEW-CRUNCH-CHEW-CRUNCH-CHEW! It gives him the chills. He shakes it off and yells down to Rudy and Bethany as they slide him up next to the wing of the 767.

                  BRIAN
          Hold it.

They cease pushing and Brian carefully climbs down the ladder until his head is on level with the underside of the Delta`s jet wing. Both the 767 and 727 are equipped with single-port fueling ports in the left wing.

He is now looking at a small square hatch with words FUEL TANK ACCESS and CHECK

SHUT-OFF VALVE BEFORE REFUELING stenciled across it. In the meantime, Albert, Bob, and Nick have pushed the hose cart driven by Laurel into position below him, and are now looking up, their faces dirty grey circles in the brightening gloom. Brian leans over and shouts down to Nick.

                    BRIAN
          There are two hoses, one
          on either side of the
          cart! I want the short
          one!

Nick pulls it free and hands it up. Holding both the ladder and the nozzle with one hand, Brian leans under the wing and opens the refueling hatch. Inside is a male connector with a steel prong poking out like a finger. Brian leans further out -- and slips. He grabs the railing of the ladder just in time. Nick leaps up the ladder, two steps at a time.

                    NICK
          Hold on, mate.

He stops three rungs below Brian, and seizes his belt. Brian leans out again, using both hands now that Nick has him fully anchored, and slams the nozzle into the fuel port. There is a brief spattering shower of jet-fuel, and then a hard metallic click. He pulls himself back onto the ladder with a deep breath. Nick shouts in his ear.

                    NICK
          What now, mate?

                    BRIAN
          I`m going to use the
          auxiliary power units on
          our plane to suck the
          fuel out of the 727.

                    NICK
          How long is it going to
          take?

                    BRIAN
          I don`t know. At least an
          hour. Maybe two.

Nick gazes anxiously eastward for a moment,
and when he speaks again, his voice is
low.

                    NICK
          You better hustle it up,
          mate. I don`t think we
          have two hours. We may
          not even have one.

He nods toward the east.

The sound coming from that direction is
louder now and closer.

And hungrier.

CHEW-CRUNCH-CHEW CRUNCH-CHEW!

INT. 767 -FIRST CLASS COMPARTMENT - DAY

Dinah lays in the stretcher, breathing shallowly, looking more dead than alive. Her sightless eyes suddenly pop open.

She raises a blood-stained hand as though reaching for someone and whispers hoarsely.

                    DINAH
          Craig.

INT. LOWER LOBBY - DAY

Craig Toomy lays on the floor with his bloody face. He stirs with a groan, throwing up a hand as though to ward something off.

Dinah`s voice reverberates inside his head.

                    DINAH (V.O.)
          Craig. Get up, Craig.

He rolls to one side with a moan.

                    TOOMY
          Let me die, oh, please,
          just let me die.

Her voice comes again, more insistent this time.

                    DINAH (V.O.)
          Craig, you have to get
          up! Now!

> TOOMY
> Go away. I hate you. Go
> away.

He buries his face in his hands, refusing to move, trying not to listen.

INT. 767 - DAY

Dinah summons what little of her strength remains and speaks again, louder this time.

> DINAH
> Craig, they`ve come to
> you -- all the people you
> wanted to see. They left
> Boston and came here. You
> can still see them, Craig
> -- if you`re man enough
> to get up, that is.

INT. LOWER LOBBY - DAY

Craig Toomy`s eyes snap open, his face suffusing with righteous indignation.

> TOOMY
> Man enough? <u>Man</u> enough?
> Whoever you are, you`ve
> <u>got</u> to be kidding me.

He wipes the blood from his face and raises his head. There, in a corona of light directly ahead of him near the luggage conveyor belt, stands Dinah. Her dark glasses are gone and she is looking at him with kind eyes as she speaks.

> DINAH
> Come on, Craig. They
> won`t wait forever. The
> Langoliers will see to
> that.

He raises his head further to see that she is not standing on the floor; rather her shoes appear to float an inch or two above it, and the bright light is all around her. She is outlined in spectral radiance. She smiles at him, holding out a glowing hand.

> DINAH
> Come, Craig. Get up.

He struggles to his feet, falling back twice before he makes it. He stands there, staring at the vision, weaving on his feet.

> DINAH
> This way, Craig. They are
> all waiting. For you.

The vision turns toward the conveyor belt. Craig Toomy, bloody face and all, starts staggering after her.

INT. PLANE - FIRST CLASS COMPARTMENT - DAY

Dinah falls back onto the stretcher, dark puddles of exhaustion pooling under her eyes. She stares at nothing and whispers to herself.

                    DINAH
          I`m sorry, Mr. Toomy. In
          spite of what you did,
          I`m sorry. But we need
          you. So, please, hurry,
          hurry!

INT. COCKPIT - DAY

Brian sits in front of the control board,
Nick beside him. The APUs work, sucking
the 727`s fuel tanks dry. As Brian
watches, the LED readout on his right tank
slowly climbs toward 24,000 pounds when
he suddenly hears the steady whine of the
small jet engines at the rear of the plane
change. They grow rough and labored. Nick
throws him a glance.

                    NICK
          What is it, mate?

Brian frowns back.

                    BRIAN
          The APU engines are
          getting a taste of the
          727`s fuel and they don`t
          like it.

Just before the LED readout in the right
tank reaches 26,000 pounds, the first APU
cuts out. A red ENGINE SHUTDOWN light
appears on the board. Brian flicks the
APU off. Nick rises, looking over Brian`s

shoulder.

                    NICK
          What can you do about it?

                    BRIAN
          Use the other three APUs
          to keep the pumps running
          and hope.

The second APU cuts out a second later, and
as Brian moves his hand to shut it down,
the third goes. The cockpit lights go with
it; now there is only the irregular chug
of the hydraulic pumps and the flickering
lights on Brian`s board. The last APU roars
choppily, cycling up and down, shaking the
plane with a nasty vibration. Brian shakes
his head hopelessly.

                    BRIAN
          I`m shutting down
          completely. We`ll have to
          wait for the Delta`s fuel
          to join our plane`s time
          stream --

But as Brian reaches for the switch, the
engine`s choppy note begins to smooth out.
His hand freezes and he turns and looks at
Nick unbelievingly. Nick looks back, a big
slow grin lighting his face.

                    NICK
          We may have lucked out,
          mate.

Brian raises a hand and crosses his fingers for luck and flicks the switches marked APU 1, 3, and 4. They kick in smoothly. The cockpit lights flash back on.

The cabin bells bing. Nick whoops and claps Brian on the back. Brian grins back as Bethany appears in the open doorway behind them, looking at them.

> BETHANY
> What`s happening? Is
> everything all right?

Brian turns his grin on her.

> BRIAN
> I think we might just
> have a shot at this
> thing.

INT. TERMINAL -LOWER LOBBY - DAY

Craig Toomy staggers to a halt, staring at the glowing girl.

She now floats with her feet just above the luggage conveyor belt, looking at him with supernatural sweetness. He smiles at her, mad hope flickering across his face.

> TOOMY
> <u>You</u> brought them to me,
> didn`t you? The chairman
> of the board, the company
> directors, all of them.

                    DINAH
          Yes. But you have to
          hurry, Craig. You have to
          hurry before they decide
          you`re not coming and
          leave.

Toomy begins to move his way forward
slowly.

Dinah`s feet do not move, but she floats
backward like a mirage, toward the rubber
strips which hang between the luggage-
retrieval area and the loading dock
outside.

And she is smiling, a huge, glorious smile
that promises both peace and redemption.

EXT. 727 - DAY

Everyone is on the plane now, except for
Bob and Albert who stand at the bottom of
the stairs, listening to the CRUNCH CHEW-
CRUNCH-WHINE sound roll toward them.

It is close, very, very close now.

INT. 727 - DAY

Laurel stands just inside the open door,
staring out across the runway, looking
eastward and listening to what she cannot
yet see.

Bethany appears behind her, yelling to

make herself heard above the chugging APUs
and the approaching Langoliers.

                    BETHANY
          Dinah is talking in her
          sleep, or something.
          I think she might be
          delirious.

Laurel turns, following Bethany to the
middle of the first class compartment where
Rudy sits across from Dinah, holding one
of her hands and peering at her anxiously.
He looks up worriedly as they approach.

                     RUDY
          I dunno, but maybe she`s
          slipping away.

Laurel feels the girl`s forehead.

It is dry, but her respiration comes in
a series of pitiful whispering sounds and
blood is caked around her mouth.

                    LAUREL
          I think --

Dinah suddenly speaks, quite clearly and
urgently.

                    DINAH
          You have to hurry before
          they decide you`re not
          coming. You <u>have</u> to.

Rudy shoots Laurel a glance.

                    RUDY
          I think she`s dreaming
          about that guy Toomy. She
          said his name once.

Dinah speaks again, her eyes closed, but
her head moves, and she appears to listen.

                    DINAH
          Yes. Yes, I will if you
          want me to. But hurry. I
          know it hurts, but you
          <u>have</u> to hurry.

                    BETHANY
          She <u>is</u> delirious, isn`t
          she?

Laurel stares at the grievously wounded
blind girl, slowly shaking her head.

                    LAUREL
          No, I don`t think so.
          I think it might have
          something to do with --

                    BETHANY
          With what?

                    LAUREL
          With what she told Mr.
          Hopewell about Mr. Toomy.
          That -- we <u>need</u> him.
            (a beat, then abruptly)
          Leave her alone and let
          her sleep.

She turns back for the doorway. Bethany looks at Rudy miserably.

> BETHANY
> God, I hope we take off soon.

He manages a faint smile and puts an arm around her shoulder.

INT. LOWER LOBBY - DAY

Toomy reaches the conveyor belt and falls onto it with a crash. Fighting his pain, he slowly raises his head, hair hanging in his eyes, and looks at Dinah. She sits cross legged in front of the rubber strips, floating an inch off the conveyor belt. He croaks at her.

> TOOMY
> Thank you for bringing them to me. This is my last chance to be free, you see. My last chance to break away from my father and everything else.

> DINAH
> Yes, I know, but you have to hurry. Please, please, hurry.

Joy sweeps his face, blotting out the pain. His vision blurs and tears begin to run down his cheeks.

                    TOOMY
          Yes. Anything you say,
          anything --

He begins to crawl toward her, Dinah
floating back as he approaches. It only
makes him move faster.

EXT. 727 - DAY

A large, cracking sound suddenly fills the
freakish morning air.

At the bottom of the stairs, Bob and Albert
turn eastward, faces pallid and filled
with dread.

                    ALBERT
          What was that?

                    BOB
          I think it was a tree.

                    ALBERT
          But there`s no wind.

Bob licks dry lips and nods.

                    BOB
          No, there`s no wind.

The noise has now become a moving barricade
of splintered sounds. Parts of it seem to
come into focus -- and then drop back again
just before identification is possible.
Barking is heard, then yaps swallowed by a
brief sour humming like evil electricity.

The only constants are the crunching and steady drilling whine. Bethany appears in the doorway above them. She yells down, trying to make herself heard over the deafening noise.

                    BETHANY
          What`s happening?

                    ALBERT
          Nothin --

Bob seizes his shoulder and points.

                    BOB
          Look! Look over there!

Far to the east of them, on the horizon, a series of power pylons march north and south across a high wooded ridge. As Albert looks, one of the pylons totters like a toy and then falls over, pulling a snarl of power cables after it. A moment later another pylon goes, and another, and another.

                    ALBERT
          That`s not all either.
          Look at the trees. The
          trees over there are
          shaking like shrubs.

As Albert and Bob watch, the trees begin to shake, fall over, and disappear. Crunch, smack, crunch, thud, BARK! Crunch, smack, BARK! Thump, crunch. Bob grabs Albert with both hands. His eyes are huge, avid with idiotic terror.

> BOB
>> We have to get out of
>> here. We have to get out
>> of here _right now_!

On the horizon, the tall gantry of a radio tower trembles, rolls outward, and crashes down to disappear into the quaking trees.

Now they can feel the very earth beneath their feet begin to vibrate. In the doorway above them, Bethany presses her hands to her ears and screams.

> BETHANY
>> Make it stop! _Oh, please,_
>> _make it STOP_!

But the sound-wave rolls on toward them -- the crunching, smacking, eating sound of the Langoliers.

INT. COCKPIT - DAY

Brian continues to fine tune his controls. Nick looks at him tightly.

> NICK
>> Time is getting short,
>> Brian. How much longer?

Brian glances down at his fuel readouts. 27,000 pounds in the right wing, 16,000 pounds in the left.

                    BRIAN
          Fifteen minutes.

                    NICK
          You can`t cut that?
          You`re sure you can`t cut
          that?

Brian shakes his head and turns back to
his gauges.

ACT 4

EXT. TERMINAL -LUGGAGE-LOADING AREA -
DAY

Craig Toomy crawls through the rubber
strips and emerges into the white, dead
light of a new and vastly foreshortened day.
The sound is terrible now, overwhelming,
that of an invading cannibal army. Dinah
turns in front of him and points eastward
beyond the American Pride 767. There, in
a triangle of dead grass bounded by two
runways, <u>is a long mahogany boardroom
table</u>. It gleams brightly in the listless
light. At each place is a yellow legal
pad, a pitcher of water, and a Waterford
glass. Sitting around the table are two
dozen men in sober banker`s suits. They
all turn as one to look at Craig Toomy.
Suddenly they begin to clap their hands.
They stand and face him. A huge, grateful
grin begins to stretch Toomy`s face.

INT. 767 -FIRST CLASS COMPARTMENT - DAY

Laurel and Rudy look up as Dinah`s breathing
becomes labored, and her voice a strangled
choke.

                    DINAH
          Run to them, Craig!
          Quick! Quick!

EXT. LUGGAGE LOADING AREA - DAY

Craig tumbles off the conveyor, strikes the concrete with a bone-rattling thump, and flails to his feet. The corona around the floating image of Dinah begins to dim, and she fades out, but it no longer matters to Toomy. His gaze is on the boardroom table and the men around it. Dinah`s fading voice reaches his mind.

                    DINAH (V.O.)
          Run to them, Craig! Run
          around the plane! Run
          away from the plane! Run
          to them now!

Toomy begins to run in a long shambling stride like a crippled sprinter.

INT. COCKPIT - DAY

The LED readout on the control board reaches 30,000 pounds, and Brian quickly flicks two switches, shutting down the hydraulic pumps.

He stands, glancing at Nick.

                    BRIAN
          All right. We`re
          uncoupling and getting
          the hell out of here.

Nick rises to join him when Bethany suddenly screams from the first class cabin.

                    BETHANY (O.S.)
          Mr. Toomy! It`s Mr.
          Tommy!

Nick dives for the door, Brian right behind
him.

INT. FIRST CLASS CABIN - DAY

They reach the open doorway, staring out
past Bethany, Rudy, and Laurel just in time
to see Craig Toomy shambling and lurching
across the taxiway. He ignores the plane
completely, his destination seeming to be
an empty triangle of grass bounded by a
pair of criss-crossing taxiways.

                    RUDY
          What`s he doing?

                    BRIAN
          Never mind him! We`re all
          out of time!

EXT. 727 - DAY

He and Nick leap down the ladder, helping
Albert and Bob roll it back into place
beneath the overlapping wings. Nick and
Brian race back up the ladder, Nick holding
Brian`s belt again as the pilot leans out
and twists the nozzle out of the hatch,
unlocking it. He then yanks the hose free
and drops it to the cement. Brian slams
the fuel-port door shut. Nick pulls him
back. Brian looks at him, his face a dirty
grey.

                    BRIAN
          Come on. Let`s get out of
          here.

But Nick does not move. He is frozen in
place, staring to the east.

His upper lip trembles and his face has
gone the color of paper.

Brian turns his head slowly in the same
direction.

They watch as the Langoliers finally enter
stage left, rolling out of the trees and
across the ground toward the runway, still
too distant to be made out clearly, but
obviously a sea of something moving rapidly
in their direction.

EXT. TRIANGLE OF GRASS - DAY

Craig Toomy stops behind the empty chair
at the head of the table. The men all sit
down except for TOM HOLBY, 50 plus, the
chairman of the board.

                    TOM HOLBY
          So give us your report,
          Craig. Tell us how much
          money you made for us.

A crazy grin tugs at Toomy`s lips. He`s
getting ready to pull the pin and self-
destruct at last.

                    TOOMY
          Yes, of course. The money
          I made for you. Well, you
          see --

His father must know it, too, because his
VOICE suddenly thunders inside Craig`s
head.

                    ROGER TOOMY (V.O.)
          No, Craig! Tell them
          you lost the money, but
          it was a mistake, an
          accident --

Toomy shakes his head, trying to ignore
the voice, and suddenly screams into the
shocked faces of the men watching him.

                    TOOMY
          I didn`t make any money
          at all! In fact, I lost
          it! I lost all forty
          three million dollars of
          your money and I did it
          deliberately! Do you hear
          me? I did it deliberately!

His father suddenly steps out from behind
Tom Holby, staring at him furiously.

                    ROGER TOOMY
          You fool! You stupid
          fool! Now I`m going to
          let them have you!

Toomy stares back at his father defiantly.

                    TOOMY
          You don`t frighten me
          anymore, father! There
          are no such things as
          Langoliers! You just made
          them up!

A dry whickering SOUND, like a thousand
buzz saws chewing through plaster, suddenly
distracts him, and he looks around, but
sees nothing. He turns his attention back
to his father and the table only to see
they are gone. He stares at the empty patch
of grass, speaking in a small perplexed
whisper.

                    TOOMY
          Where am I?

Then he hears that dry whickering SOUND
again, closer now, and turns, looking
Eastward, and finally he sees them. The
Langoliers. And they are coming. A sea
of them. For him. Craig Toomy begins to
scream.

EXT. 767 - DAY

Brian and Nick still stand on the ladder,
trying to make the shapes which have begun
to appear at the east end of Runway 21
into something they can understand. At
first there are only two, one black, one
a dark tomato red. They look like cannon
balls, but balls which ripple and contract
and then expand again, as if they`re
seeing them through a heat-haze. They

come shooting out of the high dead grass at the end of Runway 21, leaving narrow cut swaths of perfect gleaming blackness behind them, as though they are somehow cutting the grass.

They continue racing down the white concrete at the end of the runway, leaving narrow dark tracks behind them. They glisten like wet tar. There is something malignantly joyful about their behavior. They criss-cross each other`s paths, leaving a wavering black X on the outer taxiway. They bound high in the air, do an exuberant criss-crossing maneuver, and then shoot straight for the plane, the glittering black tracks trailing behind them.

Both Nick and Brian scream at the same time because they suddenly see what lurks beneath the surfaces of the racing cannon balls. Faces! Monstrous, alien faces.

They shimmer and twist, their eyes only rudimentary indentations, but the mouths are huge: circular caves lined with gnashing, blurring teeth which seem to devour everything in their path.

They eat as they come, rolling up narrow strips of the world. A Texaco fuel truck is parked on the outer taxiway, directly in the path of the on-rushing wave. As the two men watch, the Langoliers whip through it. High-speed teeth whir and crunch and bulge out of their blurred bodies. One of them burrows a path directly through the rear tires. Brian can see the shape it has cut -- a shape like a cartoon mouse-hole in a cartoon baseboard -- and then the tires collapse.

The others leap high, disappearing for a moment behind the Texaco truck`s boxy tank, and then blast straight through, leaving a metal-ringed hole from which high octane gas sprays in an amber flood. The cannon balls strike the ground, shoot upward as if jet propelled, then dart ahead, criss-crossing again in a trail of gleaming black, and race toward the plane. Brian and Nick stand on the ladder, for the moment too terrified to move.

The Langoliers reach the edge of the tarmac and pause. They jitter in place for a moment, as though they are trying to decide between the plane or Craig Toomy, who stands in the dead patch of grass, looking their way and screaming his lungs out. He suddenly bolts and starts running madly for the terminal and the Langoliers turn just as suddenly and zip after him.

Toomy runs right in front of the parked planes, Bob and Albert at the bottom of the rolling ladder and Nick and Brian 727, at the top, the others in the open doorway of the all watching, equally terrified, as the Langoliers tear past, ignoring them as they pursue Toomy. With a huge effort, Brian snaps the paralysis that grips him and elbows Nick who is still frozen below him.

                    BRIAN
              Come on, move it!

They dive down the stairway and with
Albert and Bob`s help push it back to the
doorway of the plane. All four bound up the
stairway and into the plane as more black
and red cannon balls appear at the edge of
the tarmac. They bounce, dance, circle --
and then race toward Craig Toomy, leaving
those wet black tracks behind.

EXT. RUNWAY - TRIANGLE OF GRASS - DAY

Craig Toomy runs for the terminal for all
he`s worth, casting horrified, grimacing
looks behind him. His father`s voice echoes
inside his head.

                    ROGER TOOMY (V.O.)
              No, Craig. You may THINK
              you`re running, but
              you`re not. You know what
              you`re really doing --
              you`re SCAMPERING!

Behind him, two cannon ball shapes speed
up, closing the gap with effortless speed.
They criss-cross twice, leaving spiky lines
of blackness behind them. They dart toward
Craig about seven inches apart, creating
what look like negative ski tracks behind
their weird, shimmering bodies.

They catch him twenty feet from the

luggage conveyor belt and chew his feet off in a millisecond. At one moment, his briskly scampering feet are there. At the next, Craig Toomy is three inches shorter; his feet, along with his expensive Bally loafers, simply cease to exist. Craig crashes to the ground as the Langoliers bank in a tight turn and rush at him again. He screams.

                    TOOMY
          No! No, Daddy! No! I`ll
          be good! I SWEAR I`LL BE
          GOOD FROM NOW ON IF YOU
          JUST MAKE THEM GO AW --

They rush toward him, gibbering, yammering, buzzing, whining, and he sees the frozen blur of their gnashing teeth in the half second before they cut him apart.

EXT. 767 - DAY

Laurel stands at the open door as the jet engines scream and Brian pulls the plane away from the ladder and wing of the Delta jet, watching the Langoliers cut Craig Toomy into small bits. She is about to throw up when suddenly Nick appears behind her, jerks her back, and slams the forward door shut.

INT. 767 - DAY

Nick dogs the door down and puts his arms around Laurel as she buries her burning, shocked face into the hollow of his neck.

INT. COCKPIT - DAY

Brian powers up as fast as he can, and sends the 767 charging along the runway at a suicidal rate of speed.

EXT. 767 - RUNWAY - DAY

The plane continues to accelerate. The eastern edge of the airport is now black and red with invading balls. In that direction the white, unmoving sky marches over a world of scrawling black lines and fallen trees. The jet picks up speed, roaring toward the end of the runway.

INT. COCKPIT - DAY

Brian picks up the microphone and shouts into it.

> BRIAN
> Belt in! Belt in!

Outside his window he suddenly sees two Langoliers slash across the runway in front of him, leaving black lines twenty yards apart. The entire section of runway caves in and falls away, leaving nothing behind but a yawning black chasm. Brian screams, unable to believe his eyes, and slews the 767 right onto Runway 33.

INT. MAIN COMPARTMENT - DAY

Everybody is belted down or fumbling

desperately to do so as the plane goes into its slashing turn. They are whipped left, then hard to the right.

EXT. RUNWAY - DAY

The 767 completes its 180 degree turn and jerks to a halt, its nose pointed West, down runway 33, lying open and deserted in front of it.

INT. MAIN CABIN - DAY

Overhead compartments burst open with the sudden stop and carry-on luggage is sprayed across the compartment in a deadly hail. Bethany, who is still trying to fasten her seat belt, is hurled into Albert`s lap.

Albert grabs her as an attaché case caroms off the curved wall three feet in front of his nose.

INT. COCKPIT - DAY

Brian powers the jets up for takeoff. As he does so, he sees something out the window that makes his mind cringe and wail even more: huge sections of the terminal which lays to his right, huge sections of the runway in front of it, huge sections of _reality itself_, are falling into the ground like freight elevators, leaving big senseless chunks of emptiness behind.

INT. MAIN CABIN - DAY

Albert and the others crowd the windows on the right side, looking out on the terminal. They watch the dark speeding 21, and the glistening black shapes slashing across Runway tracks they leave behind. They converge in a giant well of blackness where the luggage-unloading area and Craig Toomy had so recently been. Bethany rights herself, looking at Albert.

> BETHANY
> What is it?

Albert nods out the window at the growing blackness the Langoliers leave behind.

> ALBERT
> They`re being drawn to
> Mr. Toomy. Or to where
> Mr. Toomy was.

In front of them, seated next to Nick, Laurel suddenly speaks, her voice filled with wonder.

> LAUREL
> If he hadn`t come out of
> the terminal, they would
> have eaten the plane --
> and us inside it -- from
> the wheels up.

She and Nick exchange glances and turn as one to look at Dinah strapped to her stretcher. Nick whispers under his breath.

                    NICK
          She knew. Somehow she
          knew --

INT. COCKPIT - DAY

Brian cycles the jets up, glancing down
at the gauge that tells him when he has
reached full power. Not yet.

He turns, staring out the window as the
terminal continues to be sliced and diced
by what now seems like thousands of black
and red balls.

INT. MAIN CABIN - DAY

Bob tears his eyes from the window and
leans forward, speaking to the others in
a trembling, awed voice.

                    BOB
          Now we know, don`t we?

Laurel twists in her seat, looking back
at him as Nick lets go of her and raises
his head.

                    LAUREL
          What? What do we know?

                    BOB
          Why, what happens to
          today when it becomes
          yesterday. It waits --
          for _them_.

He nods out the windows where the Langoliers continue to chew up the terminal, pieces crashing into the blackness and leaving nothing behind but more blackness.

                    BOB
          It waits for the time-
          keepers of eternity,
          always running along
          behind, cleaning up
          the mess in the most
          efficient way possible --
          by eating it.

Dinah suddenly speaks up from her stretcher in a clear, dreaming voice.

                    DINAH
          Mr. Toomy knew about
          them. Mr. Toomy said they
          were the Langoliers.

They all look at her, stunned that she spoke, as the jet engines continue to roar faster and faster outside the windows.

INT. COCKPIT - DAY

Brian glances at his gauge. The jets still aren`t up to full power. He glances out the window. Two Langoliers suddenly leave the terminal, racing in the direction of the plane, leaving those glistening black tracks behind. As Brian continues to watch horrified, more of the balls follow the first two. He glances down at the gauge. Not yet, dammit, not yet!

EXT. PLANE -RUNWAY - DAY

A horde of Langoliers now zip toward the plane, still parked at the top of runway 33, its engines faster and faster.

INT. COCKPIT - DAY

The gauge reach full power. A row of lights on the control board turn from red to green. Brian pops the brake, and shoves the throttle full forward.

EXT. RUNWAY - DAY

The plane leaps ahead, charging down Runway 33, the Langoliers only milliseconds behind, curving to follow them, eating the runway up behind them.

INT. COCKPIT - DAY

Brian leans down on the throttle, shoving it forward even more, cranking the engine to the max.

EXT. 767 - DAY

Two of the Langoliers break out of the pack chasing the airplane, and speed ahead, quickly cutting the distance.

INT. 767 - MAIN CABIN - DAY

Bethany stares out the window, sees one of

the Langoliers come into view alongside, and screams. Albert leans over, looking out.

EXT. RUNWAY - DAY

A black ball speeds alongside the 767, then another one, both chewing up the edge of the runway, pacing the jet. Suddenly they pulls ahead and jag to the left toward the front of the plane.

INT. COCKPIT - DAY

Brian watches horrified as the two Langoliers cut in front of the charging plane.

EXT. RUNWAY - DAY

They dig double parallel trenches directly in front of the wheels of the racing jet.

INT. COCKPIT - DAY

They hit the trenches and Brian is snapped upward in his chair, the safety harness grabbing him and slamming him back down.

INT. MAIN CABIN - DAY

There is a terrific bump that lifts them all out of their seats.

Rudy looks around wildly, shouting.

> RUDY
> Did it get us? Did it get
> us?!

No one answers. They are too busy staring out the various windows with their pale, terrified faces.

INT. COCKPIT - DAY

Brian leans forward, staring out at the blackness rushing toward him a 150 yards in front where the runway ends and trying to comprehend it. Suddenly a Langolier slices through it and 75 more yards gives way, falling into the growing chasm of black nothingness. Stifling an involuntary scream as he sees his takeoff distance suddenly, literally, cut in half, he hauls back on the yoke with all his strength.

EXT. RUNWAY - DAY

The plane tears down the runway for the black chasm, trying to lift off, but failing.

INT. COCKPIT - DAY

Brian looks down at his speedometer. 120 miles an hour, still 30 miles an hour short of the speed he needs for lift-off. Out the cockpit window, the black chasm rushes toward him. He pulls back on the yoke harder, silently willing the plane to rise with all his might.

EXT. RUNWAY - DAY

The 767 lifts off the ground seconds before
it reaches the end of the runway and the
black abyss beyond it.

INT. MAIN CABIN - DAY

Rudy stands up, looking out the window
across the aisle, shouting wildly at his
fellow travellers.

                    RUDY
          Did we make it? Are we
          off the ground

INT. COCKPIT - DAY

Brian`s eyes widen with terror as all he
sees out the cockpit window is blackness
with nothing to give him any bearing.

He pulls back on the yoke and banks sharply
to the right.

EXT. SKY - DAY

The plane goes into a sudden bank, turning
right over the terminal in a wide swooping
curve.

INT. MAIN CABIN - DAY

Rudy is hurled off his feet into a row of
empty seats three quarters of the way up
the cabin.

He rights himself and looks at the others
with a wide, frightened gaze.

                    RUDY
          What happened? Are we
          crashing?

Nick speaks without taking his eyes off
the view out the window.

                    NICK
          Buckle yourself in, mate,
          and shut u --

He breaks off, staring incredulously down
at the airport - or where the airport had
been.

EXT. AIRPORT - DAY

Only the main buildings of the airport and
a constantly diminishing patch of ground
around it, runways and parking lots, are
left. Everything else has already been
eaten. Flight 29 slowly turns West and
overflies a growing abyss of darkness, an
eternal cistern that seems to have no end.

INT. 767 - DAY

Laurel peers over Nick`s shoulder and
speaks unsteadily.

                    LAUREL
          Oh, dear Jesus, Nick.

She puts her hands over her face, no longer able to bear what she is seeing. Nick`s eyes remain fastened out the window on the terminal below as they hit 1,500 feet, still climbing.

EXT. RUNWAY 33 - DAY

Sixty to a hundred parallel lines race up, over, and across the terminal and the surrounding runway and buildings, cutting them into long strips that sink into nothingness.

INT. 767 - DAY

Bethany abruptly tears her eyes from the window and pulls down the shade beside Albert with a bang.

                    BETHANY
          Don`t you dare open that!

Albert pulls back from the window, nods jerkily, understanding just how she feels.

                    ALBERT
          Don`t worry, I won`t.

INT. COCKPIT - DAY

Brian pulls on the yoke and twists. The plane begins to bank west again, but not before he glances out the window and sees what lays to the east of airport where Bangor should be.

EXT. EAST OF BANGOR - DAY

<u>Nothing</u> lays east of Bangor. Nothing at all, not even Bangor.

A titanic river of blackness lays in a still sweep from horizon to horizon under the white dome of the sky. The trees are gone, the city is gone, the terminal is gone, the earth itself is gone.

INT. COCKPIT - DAY

Brian`s mouth falls open as he tries to hang on to his sanity.

                    BRIAN
          Oh, my God --

Brian straightens the yoke and pulls up higher, sending the plane rising for the clouds above.

EXT. SKY - DAY

The plane disappears into the clouds.

INT. MAIN CABIN - DAY

Bob stares out the dim interior of the plane at the dirty whiteness of the clouds outside.

Suddenly they burst into the bright-blue world which begins at 18,000 feet.

The remaining passengers look at each other nervously as Brian comes on the intercom.

                    BRIAN (V.O.)
          We`re up. You all know
          what happens now: we go
          back exactly the way we
          came in, and hope that
          whatever doorway we came
          through is still there.
          If it is, we`ll try going
          through.

He clicks off.

Nick turns to Laurel, gives her a brief hug, unbuckles his seat belt, and stands up.

                    NICK
          I`m going forward. Want
          to come?

She shakes her head and points across the aisle at Dinah.

                    LAUREL
          I`ll stay with her.

He brushes at her hair gently with the palm of his hand.

                    NICK
          We have a dinner date --
          you haven`t forgotten,
          have you?

                    LAUREL
          No. I haven`t and I
          won`t.

He bends down and brushes a kiss lightly
across her mouth.

                    NICK
          Neither will I.

He goes forward and she presses her fingers
lightly against her mouth, as if to hold
the kiss there, then unbuckles her seat
belt, crosses the aisle, and puts her hand
on Dinah`s forehead.

She leans forward, kissing each of Dinah`s
cool, closed lids, and whispering to her.

                    LAUREL
          Hold on. Please, hold on,
          Dinah.

Across the aisle, Bethany turns to Albert,
holding both of his hands in hers.

                    BETHANY
          What happens if the fuel
          goes bad?

Albert looks at her seriously and kindly.

                    ALBERT
          You know the answer to
          that, Bethany.

She fumbles out her cigarettes, looks up

at the NO SMOKING sign and puts them away
again.

                    BETHANY
          Yeah, I know. We crash.
          End of story.
                    (a beat, then)
          Would you like to kiss
          me?

                    ALBERT
          Yes.

                    BETHANY
          Well, you better go
          ahead, then. The later it
          gets, the later it gets.

Albert goes ahead.

EXT. SKY -FORTY MINUTES LATER

The blue sky through which Flight 29 moves
begins to deepen in color.

It cycles slowly to indigo, and then to
deep purple as twilight falls.

INT. COCKPIT - DAY INTO NIGHT

Brian looks up from his instruments,
checking out the darkening sky outside.

Nick slips through the door and into the
seat beside him.

He follows his gaze out the window.

                    NICK
          It`s going faster, isn`t
          it?

Brian turns to face him.

                    BRIAN
          Yes, it is. After awhile
          the "days" and "nights"
          will be passing as fast
          as a camera shutter can
          click, I think.
               (a beat, then)
          We were all going to
          Boston for different
          reasons. What about you,
          Nick? 'Fess up. The hour
          groweth late.

Nick looks at him thoughtfully for a moment
and then laughs.

                    NICK
          Well, why not. What
          does a Most Secret
          classification mean when
          you`ve just seen a bunch
          of killer cannon balls
          rolling up the world.

He laughs again.

                    NICK
          I`m a Special Operator in
          the armed services,

                    NICK (CONT.)
          Brian. I do various odd
          jobs, some innocuous,
          some fabulously nasty.

Full darkness falls outside now.

The stars gleam like spangles on a woman`s
formal evening gown.

                         NICK
          There`s a man in Boston,
          you see - or was -- or
          will be -- who is a
          politician of some note.
          This man - I`ll call him
          Mr. O`Banion, for the
          sake of conversation --
          is very rich, Brian, and
          he is an enthusiastic
          supporter of the Irish
          Republican Army. He is
          also an idealist of the
          most dangerous sort: one
          who has never had to view
          the carnage at first
          hand, and been forced to
          reconsider his actions in
          light of that experience.

                        BRIAN
          You were supposed to kill
          this man?

                        NICK
          Not unless I had to. He
          has a great many powerful

                    NICK (CONT.)
          American friends, and
          some of his friends are
          our friends. Therefore
          killing Mr. O`Banion would
          be a great political
          risk. But he keeps a
          little bit of fluff on
          the side. She was the one
          I was supposed to kill.

                    BRIAN
          As a warning?

                    NICK
          Yes. As a warning.

Brian stares at him, shocked. The only
sound in the cabin is the steady drone of
jet engines.

                    BRIAN
          If you get out of this,
          if we get back, will you
          carry through with it?

Nick shakes his head slowly, but with
great finality.

                    NICK
          No more midnight creeps
          for Mrs. Hopewell`s boy
          Nicholas. If we get out
          of this -- a proposition
          I find rather shaky just
          now -- I believe I`ll
          retire.

                    BRIAN
          And do what?

Nick looks at him thoughtfully for a moment
and then replies.

                    NICK
          Well -- I suppose I could
          take up flying.

Brian breaks up laughing. After a moment,
Mrs. Hopewell`s boy joins in.

EXT. SKY - NIGHT INTO DAY

Thirty-five minutes later, daylight begins
to seep back into the sky, illuminating
the wide-bodied jet.

INT. MAIN CABIN - DAY

Laurel looks up, blinking in the sudden
daylight flooding the cabin. She looks
around and sees that Dinah`s sightless
eyes are open. She reaches out and grasps
one of the girl`s hands.

                    LAUREL
          Don`t try to talk, Dinah.
          We`re going back, and
          you`re going to be all
          right -- I promise you
          that.

Dinah`s hand tightens on her, and tugs her
forward. Dinah speaks in a fading voice.

>   DINAH
>   Don`t worry about me,
>   Laurel. I got -- what I
>   wanted.

>   LAUREL
>   Dinah, you shouldn`t

The unseeing brown eyes move toward the
sound of Laurel`s voice. A little smile
touches Dinah`s bloody mouth.

>   DINAH
>   I saw. I saw through Mr.
>   Toomy`s eyes. At the
>   start, everything looked
>   mean and nasty to him,
>   but it was better at the
>   end

She coughs. Small flecks of blood fly from
her mouth.

>   LAUREL
>   Please, Dinah. Please
>   don`t try to talk
>   anymore.

Dinah smiles.

>   DINAH
>   I saw <u>you</u>. You are
>   beautiful, Laurel,
>   especially your eyes.
>   <u>Everything</u> was beautiful
>   -- even the things that
>   were dead. It was so

                    DINAH (CONT.)
              wonderful to - you know
              -- just to see.

She draws in a tiny sip of air, lets it
out, and simply doesn`t take the next one.
Her sightless eyes now seem to be looking
far beyond Laurel Stevenson. Laurel takes
the girl`s hands in hers and begins to
repeatedly kiss them.

                    LAUREL
              Please breathe, Dinah.
              Please breathe, please,
              please, please

But Dinah does not breathe. Laurel slowly
returns the girl`s hands to her lap and
looks blankly around. Across the aisle
she sees Albert and Bethany kissing,
delicately, almost religiously. Rudy sits
nearby, clutching his rosary tightly, and
Bob Jenkins stares out the window, lost
once more in thought. Laurel turns back
to Dinah, kisses the slope of her cheek
and then raises her hand to the little
girl`s face, about to close her eyes. Her
fingers stop only on inch from her eyelids
as Dinah`s voice reverberates inside her
head.

                    DINAH (V.O.)
              I saw through Mr. Toomy`s
              eyes. Everything was
              beautiful -- even the
              things that were dead. It
              was so wonderful to see.

Laurel finally speaks out loud.

                    LAUREL
          Yes, I can live with
          that.

She withdraws her hand, leaving Dinah`s
eyes open.

ACT 5

EXT. SKY -FOUR HOURS LATER - DAY

The plane suddenly clears the bank of clouds revealing where the Great Plains should be below. Only they aren`t there. Nothing is. The world below is gone; utterly and finally gone.

INT. COCKPIT - DAY INTO NIGHT

Brian stares down at the nothingness, tries to repress a shudder and fails as day begins to cycle back into night in a matter of minutes. He picks up the intercom and opens the circuit.

> BRIAN
> Nick? Can you come up
> front?

INT. MAIN CABIN - DAY INTO NIGHT

Nick looks up from where he rests, Laurel`s sleeping head against his shoulder. He quietly rises, careful not to wake her, and slips toward the front of the plane. All the others are also asleep or occupied, every window shade tightly pulled down.

INT. COCKPIT - NIGHT

Nick opens the door behind Brian and slips into the seat beside him.

                    NICK
          The little girl is gone.

Brian shakes his head sadly.

                    BRIAN
          She never got her
          operation.

                    NICK
          No.

                    BRIAN
          But Laurel is okay?

                    NICK
          More or less.

                    BRIAN
          You like her, don`t you?

                    NICK
          Yes. I have mates who
          would laugh at that, but
          I do like her. She`s got
          grit.

                    BRIAN
          Well, I wish you the
          best of luck. But right
          now I think we`d better
          concentrate on getting
          back.

Brian pulls one of his charts and lays it
out on the console. He has made a small
red circle in the left hand upper corner.

He stabs it with his finger.

                    BRIAN
          We`re just about here
          now. Where the time-rip
          should be. Will you keep
          an eye out for it while I
          fly?

Nick rises and scans the sky.

                    NICK
          Of course. I only wish I
          knew what I was looking
          <u>for</u>.

                    BRIAN
          I think you`ll know it
          when you see it. <u>If</u> you
          see it.

INT. MAIN CABIN - NIGHT

Bob sits with his hands folded tightly
across his chest, as if he is cold. His
face is creased in a troubled frown.
Ahead of him, Bethany and Albert spoon
contentedly. Behind him, Rudy sits with
his eyes closed and his lips moving. The
beads of his rosary are clamped in one
fist. Across the aisle, Laurel sits near
Dinah, silently mourning.

Bob sits farther back in his seat, his
fingers drumming on his arm rest. Something
is wrong and it`s bothering him. But what?
What is it? He abruptly unbuckles his seat

belt and stands. Albert looks up.

                    ALBERT
          What`s wrong?

                    BOB
          I don`t know and that`s
          the problem. Something <u>is</u>
          wrong. Very, very wrong.
          I just can`t figure out
          what.

He begins to walk down the aisle toward
the tail of the aircraft. Albert looks
after him.

INT. COCKPIT - NIGHT INTO DAY

Brian tears his eyes from the sky -- which
is already showing signs of daylight again
-- long enough to take a quick glance
first at the INS readout and then at the
red circle at the heart of his chart.
Suddenly Nick speaks beside him in an
unsteady voice, his eyes fixed out the
port window.

                    NICK
          Brian? I think I see
          something.

Brian stands, the two of them staring out
the window, their mouths agape in silent
awe.

INT. REAR OF PLANE - NIGHT INTO DAY

Bob reaches the tail of the plane, makes an about-face, and starts slowly up the aisle again, passing row after row of empty seats. He looks at the objects that lay in them and on the floor in front as he passes: purses, pairs of eyeglasses, wristwatches, a pocket watch, dental fillings --

He suddenly comes to a dead stop, his eyes widening. He stares at Rudy who somehow, miraculously, has dozed off in the middle of all this. He is sound asleep, <u>like he and all the others were when they went through the time rip</u>. The pieces fall into place inside Bob`s head. His mouth opens and he tries to scream, but no sound comes out. His throat is locked with terror.

INT. COCKPIT - DAY

Brian finally manages to croak out a few words as the blue grey of night drains away to be replaced by the grey-white dullness of another day.

> BRIAN
> Holy Christ in the
> morning.

EXT. PLANE - TIME RIP - DAY

The Time-Rip lays about ninety miles ahead, off to the starboard side of the 767`s nose by no more than seven or eight degrees.

It is a lozenge-shaped hole in reality,
but not a black void. It cycles with a
dim pink-purple light, like the Aurora
Borealis. Beyond it can be seen stars,
also rippling. A white ribbon of vapor
slowly streams into the shape which hangs
in the sky. It looks like some strange,
eternal highway.

INT. COCKPIT - DAY

Nick laughs idiotically and shakes his
clenched fists in the air.

                    NICK
          We`re in business!

Brian smiles and opens his intercom.

                    BRIAN
          Ladies and gentlemen, we
          have found what we were
          looking for.

INT. MAIN CABIN - DAY

Bob`s mouth falls open in mute horror
as he listens to Brian`s words over the
intercom.

                    BRIAN (V.O.)
          I`m going to take us
          straight through the
          middle of it and we`ll
          find out what`s on the
          other side --

Bob suddenly comes unstuck, pelting down the aisle, screaming at the top of his lungs.

> BOB
> <u>No</u>! <u>No</u>! <u>We`ll all die</u>
> <u>if you go into it</u>! <u>Turn</u>
> <u>back</u>! <u>You`ve got to turn</u>
> <u>back</u>!

INT. COCKPIT - DAY

Brian swings around in his seat and exchanges a puzzled look with Nick as they hear Bob`s muffled shouts. Nick unbuckles his belt and stands.

> NICK
> Carry on. I`ll handle
> him.

Nick slips out the door as Brian leans forward, staring at the time slip. He can now see that there are vivid flashes of color traveling within it: green, blue, violet, red, candy pink.

It`s the first real color he`s seen in these lead grey clouds. He pulls backward on the yoke and to the right.

EXT. SKY - DAY

The plane tilts gently up and away as it banks toward the long glowing slot ahead.

INT. FIRST-CLASS SECTION - DAY

Bob bursts into first class from the main cabin, racing down the narrow aisle and right into Nick`s waiting arms.

                    NICK
          Easy, mate. Everything`s
          gonna be all right now.

Bob struggles wildly, yelling as loud as he can.

                    BOB
          No! No, you don`t
          understand! He`s got to
          turn back! He`s got to
          turn back before it`s too
          late!

Nick pulls the screaming writer away from the cockpit door and into first class, forcing him into a seat.

INT. COCKPIT - DAY

In here Bob`s voice is just a faint blur of sound as Brian adjusts the yolk.

EXT. PLANE -TIME-RIP - DAY

The 767 enters the wide flow of vapor streaming into the Time-Rip, heading directly for the lozenge-shaped hole in the sky.

INT. FIRST-CLASS CABIN - DAY

Nick tries to hold a terrified Bob down
and fasten his seat belt as the older man
shrieks at him.

                    BOB
          We were all asleep when
          we came through, you
          damn fool! Don`t you
          understand? WE WERE
          ASLEEP!

Nick freezes in the act of buckling Bob
in. What Bob is saying -- what he has been
trying to say all along -- hits him like
a dropped ton of bricks. He is suddenly
almost mute with terror.

                    NICK
          Oh, dear God --

He forgets Bob and dashes for the cockpit.

EXT. PLANE - DAY

The plane flies directly into the mouth
of the Time-Rip, its airspeed increasing
rapidly as the rip grabs hold and sucks
them through.

INT. COCKPIT - DAY

Brian steadies the yolk as Nick bursts
through the door behind him, gripping his
shoulders, staring at the rip as it swells
in front of the jet`s nose, its play of

deepening colors racing across his cheeks and brow.

> NICK
> Turn back, Brian! You
> have to turn back!

Brian reacts by instinct, grabs the steering yoke and hauls it hard over to port.

EXT. PLANE - TIME-RIP - DAY

The plane banks sharply up and away from the mouth of the Time-Rip.

INT. COCKPIT - DAY

Nick is thrown across the cockpit and into the bulkhead. There is a sickening crack as his arm breaks.

INT. FIRST CLASS - DAY

Bob grabs on to his seat, holding on for dear life, suddenly thankful that Nick belted him.

INT. MAIN CABIN - DAY

The luggage which had fallen from the overhead compartments now flies once more, striking the curved walls and thudding off the windows in a vicious hail. Bethany screams and Albert holds her tight. Two rows behind, Rudy snaps awake, closes his eyes again, clutches his rosary harder, and prays faster as his seat tilts away from him. Laurel grabs her seat, holding on for dear life as Dinah`s body sways in its stretcher beside her and bags come hurtling by.

EXT. PLANE - DAY

Now there is turbulence. Flight 29 becomes a surfboard with wings, rocketing and twisting through the unsteady air.

INT. COCKPIT - DAY

Brian is snapped upward toward the ceiling of the cockpit again. His hands are thrown off the yoke. He grabs it and opens the throttle all the way to full power.

EXT. PLANE -ENGINES - DAY

The turbines respond with a deep snarl of power rarely heard outside of an airplane`s diagnostic hangar. The turbulence increases. The plane is slammed viciously up and down. From the wings comes the deadly shriek of over stressed metal.

INT. FIRST CLASS - DAY

Bob clutches the arms of his seat, screaming in spite of himself, as the plane takes another great leap, and rocks up almost to the vertical on its port side wing.

EXT. PLANE - TIME-RIP - DAY

The turbulence continues to increase as Brian drives the 767 away from the rip and across the wide stream of vapor feeding it.

INT. COCKPIT - DAY INTO NIGHT

Brian grips the shuddering yolk harder. Ahead of him, the hole continues to swell in front of the plane`s nose even as it continues sliding off to the starboard. Then, after one particularly vicious jolt, they come out of the rapids into smoother air. The time-rip disappears to starboard. Brian continues to bank the plane, but at a less drastic angle.

Day begins to cycle once more into night.

He shouts at Nick without turning around.

> BRIAN
> Nick! Nick, are you all
> right?

Nick gets slowly to his feet, holding his right arm against his belly with his left hand. His face is very white and his teeth are set in a grimace of pain.

> NICK
> I`ve seen better, mate.
> Broke my arm. We missed
> it, didn`t we?

                    BRIAN
          We missed it. But why,
          when we came all this way
          to find it did you --

Bob steps into the cockpit before Nick can
answer. The writer is shaking, there is a
wet patch on his slacks, and his hair is
wildly disheveled.

He points to the switch marked INTERCOM as
Nick sits heavily in the co-pilot`s chair,
cradling his broken arm.

                    BOB
          Can I talk through that
          thing?

                    BRIAN
          Yes, but what the hell is
          going

Bob ignores him, picks up the mike, makes
a visible effort to compose himself, then
begins to talk.

                    BOB
          Listen to me, all of you.
          We managed to turn back
          just in time. We have
          been extremely lucky --
          and extremely stupid, as
          well. When we first went
          through the time-rip,
          everybody on the plane who
          was awake disappeared.

Brian jerks erect in his seat. He looks as if somebody had just slugged him.

Ahead of the 767`s nose, about thirty miles distant, the faintly glowing lozenge shape has appeared again in the sky, looking like some gigantic semi-precious stone.

The darkness of night grows as Bob continues talking into the intercom.

>   BOB
>   WE are all awake. Logic
>   therefore suggests that
>   if we try to go back
>   through that way, WE will
>   disappear. That is all.

Brian flicks the intercom closed without thinking about it.

Behind him, Nick voices a pained, incredulous laugh.

>   NICK
>   That is all? That is
>   bloody _all_? What do we _do_
>   about it?

Brian looks at him and doesn`t answer. Neither does Bob.

INT. MAIN CABIN - NIGHT

Bethany raises her head and looks at Albert`s strained, bewildered face.

                    BETHANY
          We have to go to sleep?
          How do we do <u>that</u>? I never
          felt less like sleeping
          in my whole life!

                     ALBERT
          I don`t know.

He looks hopefully across the aisle at
Laurel, but she is just sitting there,
shaking her head, at a loss for an answer.
Behind her, Rudy, awake now, continues to
mumble his rosary.

INT. COCKPIT - NIGHT

Bob takes a step forward and gazes out
the cockpit window at the rip in silent
fascination as Brian checks the fuel gage.
He lifts tired, helpless eyes to Nick.

                     BRIAN
          I don`t know what we do
          now, but if we`re going
          to try that hole, it has
          to be soon. The fuel
          we`ve got will carry us
          for an hour, no more.

Bob tears his eyes from the rip and looks
at him.

                      BOB
          Surely there are other
          airfields --

                    BRIAN
          There are, but none big
          enough to handle an
          airplane of this size. It
          has to be LAX and I`ll
          need at least thirty-five
          minutes to get there.
          That gives us --

He checks his chronometer.

                    BRIAN
          -- <u>twenty minutes at most</u>
          to figure this thing
          out and get through the
          hole. Now how do we put
          everybody to sleep at the
          same time?

A voice suddenly interrupts them from behind.

                    LAUREL (O.S.)
          You`re forgetting the
          most important thing of
          all, aren`t you?

They turn. Laurel, white and haggard, stands in the cockpit door.

                    LAUREL
          Even if you figure out a
          way to put us all out,
          who`s going to fly the
          plane into L.A.?

The three men gape at her wordlessly.

Behind them, unnoticed, the large semi-precious stone that is the Time-Rip glides into view again.

                    NICK
          We`re out of luck. Do you
          know that? Absolutely,
          totally dead-out of luck.

He laughs a little, then winces as his stomach jogs his broken arm.

Albert and Bethany appear in the doorway behind Laurel, looking in.

Albert has his arm around Bethany`s waist.

He looks at Brian with growing desperation.

                    ALBERT
          There has to be a way out
          of this. There has to be.
          Doesn`t there?

They all look at each other helplessly, mired in silence. Brian looks around vacantly, his gaze coming to rest on the CABIN PRESSURE dial on his control panel. His eyes slowly narrow as he remembers what happened when he first landed at LAX.

FLASH CUT - INSIDE BRIAN`S HEAD - NIGHT

Brian leans over his control board with a frown, checking the gauge that reads CABIN PRESSURE.

                    BRIAN
          Damn. This gauge doesn`t
          tell me anything. The
          leak could have been
          anywhere.

He sits back with an exhausted sigh as his
co-pilot, Danny Keene, watches him.

                    DANNY
          Don`t worry about it.
          It`s diagnostic`s problem
          now.

INT. COCKPIT - NIGHT (BACK INTO REALITY)

Brian snaps out of it, looking up at the
other, hope flashing across his face.

                    BRIAN
          There is a way out!
          Dammit, there is!

He whirls, grabbing one of his books from
the shelf where the charts are kept.

He thumbs through it wildly, looking for
something.

The others watch him.

                    NICK
          What, Brian? I can see
          you`re on to something --

Brian reads something in his book, then
looks up at them joyfully.

                    BRIAN
          Pressure. That`s what I`m
          on to. <u>Pressure</u>!

Albert`s face suddenly lights up.

                    ALBERT
          Of course! Pressure!

Nick looks wildly back and forth between
the two of them.

                    NICK
          Would you two please tell
          us what are you talking
          about?

Brian taps the rheostat on the control
board marked CABIN PRESSURE.

                    BRIAN
          I`m talking about dropping
          the air pressure in here
          to 7 psi, half sea level.
          Do that and boom, we`re
          out like lights.

He suddenly stops, all the life going out
of his face.

                    BRIAN
          Only how do we answer
          Laurel`s question? How
          do I wake up after we
          come through and land the
          plane?

They all look at each other again, the
joy leaking out of their faces. Silence
ensues. Bob breaks it, his voice dry and
toneless, like that of a judge pronouncing
doom.

                    BOB
          One of us will have to
          stay awake. One of us
          will --

His voice chokes into silence. Nick looks
at him and nods.

                    NICK
          Yes. One of us will have
          to die.

Brian looks up at their anxious face. Bob
has gone ash gray. Albert doesn`t look any
better. Neither do Bethany nor Laurel.

ACT 6

INT. COCKPIT - NIGHT

They all stare at one another, frozen into
silence.

Brian finally breaks it.

> BRIAN
> But who`s going to do it?
> Do the rest of you draw
> straws, or what?

> NICK
> No need for that. I`ll do
> it.

Laurel whirls on him. Her eyes are very
dark and very wide.

> LAUREL
> No! Why you? Why
> <u>shouldn`t</u> we draw straws?
> Why not Bob? Or Rudy? Why
> not me?

Nick takes her arm, drawing her toward the
door.

> NICK
> Come with me for a
> moment.

Brian glances at his chronometer. More
seconds have ticked past.

                    BRIAN
          Nick, there`s not much
          time left.

                    NICK
          I know. Start the things
          you have to do.

He draws Laurel through the door.

INT. FIRST CLASS GALLEY - NIGHT INTO DAY

Nick stops in the small galley alcove and
faces her.

                    NICK
          I think we might have
          something, you and me.
          Do you think I could be
          right about that? If you
          do, say so - there`s no
          time to dance. Absolutely
          none.

                    LAUREL
          Yes. I think that`s
          right.

                    NICK
          But we don`t know. We
          can`t know. It all comes
          back to time, doesn`t it?
          Time -- and sleep -- and
          not knowing. But I have
          to be the one, Laurel. I
          have tried to keep some
          reasonable account of

                    NICK (CONT.)
          myself, and all my books
          are deeply in the red.
          This is my chance to
          balance them, and I mean
          to take it.

                    LAUREL
          I don`t understand what
          you`re --

He gives her a brisk shake.

                    NICK
          I told you -- there`s no
          time to dance! Would you
          do something for me? If
          you get out of this, that
          is.

Laurel cocks her head, staring at him.

                    LAUREL
          Yes. Yes, of course.

Brian calls from the cockpit, interrupting
her.

                    BRIAN (O.S.)
          Nick!

Nick looks in that direction and shouts.

                    NICK
          Coming!
               (back to Laurel)
          Listen. Listen very

                    NICK (CONT.)
carefully. I was going to
quit it. My mind was made
up.

                    LAUREL
Quit what?

                    NICK
Doesn`t matter. What
matters is whether or not
you believe me. Do you?

                    LAUREL
Yes. I don`t know what
you`re talking about, but
I believe you mean it.

Brian bellows from the cockpit again.

                    BRIAN (O.S.)
Nick! We`re heading
toward the rip!

Nick shoots a glance toward the cockpit,
his eyes narrow and gleaming. He calls.

                    NICK
Coming just now!
          (back to Laurel)
My father lives in the
village of Fluting, south
of London. Ask for him in
any shop along the High
Street. Mr. Hopewell. The
older ones still call him
the gaffer. Go to him and

                    NICK (CONT.)
tell him I`d made up my
mind to quit it. You`ll
need to be persistent;
he tends to turn away
and curse loudly when he
hears my name. Can you be
persistent?

                    LAUREL
Yes.

He nods and smiles grimly.

                    NICK
Good! Repeat what I`ve
told you, and tell him
you believed me. Tell him
I tried my best to atone
for what happened behind
the church in Belfast.

                    LAUREL
In Belfast?

                    NICK
Right. And if you can`t
get him to listen any
other way, tell him he
<u>must</u> listen. Because of
the daisies. The time I
brought the daisies. Can
you remember that, as
well?

                    LAUREL
Because once you brought

                LAUREL (CONT.)
        him daisies.

                NICK
        No -- not to him, but
        it`ll do. Will you do it?

                LAUREL
        Yes -- but --

                NICK
        Good. Laurel, thank you.

He puts his left hand against the nape
of her neck, pulls her face to his, and
kisses her.

INT. COCKPIT - DAY

Brian finishes programing the INS computer
and rises, looking out the door for Nick.

Bethany turns scared eyes on him.

                BETHANY
        Are we going to feel
        like we`re - you know,
        choking?

Nick returns with a very shaken Laurel.

Brian drops back into his seat.

                BRIAN
        No. You`ll feel a little
        giddy - swimmy in the

                    BRIAN (CONT.)
          head -- then, nothing.
          Until we all wake up.

He glances at Nick. Nick smiles cheerfully.

                    NICK
          Right! And who knows? I
          may still be right here.
          Bad pennies have a way of
          turning up. Don`t they,
          Brian?

Brian nods, trying to match Nick`s cheerful
tone.

He pushes the throttle slightly forward.
The rip lays dead ahead.

The sky is growing bright with daylight
again.

                    BRIAN
          Anything`s possible.
                (to the others)
          Sit down, folks. Nick,
          right up here beside me.
          I`m going to show you
          what to do -- and when to
          do it.

                    LAUREL
          One second, please.

She stands on tiptoe and plants a kiss on
Nick`s mouth.

He looks at her gravely.

                    NICK
          Thank you.

                    LAUREL
          You were going to quit
          it. You`d made up your
          mind. And if he won`t
          listen, I`m to remind him
          of the day you bought the
          daisies. Have I got it
          right?

Nick grins.

                    NICK
          Letter perfect, my love.
          Letter perfect.

He encircles her with his left arm and
kisses her again, long and hard. When he
lets go, there is a gentle thoughtful
smile on his mouth.

                    NICK
          That`s the one to go on
          right enough.

                    BRIAN
          All right. Shall we?

Nick sits in the co-pilot seat and Brian
begins to explain the pressure gauge to
him. The others file out, Laurel the last
to leave.

EXT. 767 - DAY

The sun shines wanly on the plane as it
slowly circles back toward the rip.

INT. COCKPIT - DAY

Brian and Nick are alone now, each belted
into their respective seats. Brian opens
the intercom and speaks into it.

> BRIAN
> I`m starting to decrease
> pressure. Check your
> belts, everyone.

INT. MAIN CABIN - DAY

They`re all there, the small brave group
of passengers, buckling up. Albert and
Bethany sit together.

She throws him a frightened glance.

> BETHANY
> Albert, would you hold
> me, please?

> ALBERT
> Yes. If you`ll hold me.

They embrace each other as behind them Rudy
tells his Rosary again. Across the aisle,
Laurel grips the arms of her seat. She
raises her head, looking at the overhead
compartment, waiting for the masks to
fall.

Around her, the others nod off. She doesn`t
notice as she mumbles to herself with a
growing fuzziness.

                    LAUREL
          Remember about that day
          in Belfast, too. Behind
          the church. An act of
          atonement --

The air masks suddenly fall up and down
the compartment, but Laurel doesn`t see
them.

She has already drifted off.

INT. COCKPIT - DAY

Brian tries to focus on Nick who wears an
oxygen mask. Ahead of them, the Time-Rip
is once more swelling the cockpit windows,
spreading across the sky.

It is now lit with blazing sunlight, and a
fantastic new array of colors coil, swim,
and then stream away into its queer depths.

When Brian`s speaks, it is in a dreamy,
furry voice, already slipping away.

                    BRIAN
          You know -- what to do?

                    NICK
          I know. No fear, Brian.
          Off to sleep you go.
          Sweet dreams, and all

                    NICK (CONT.)
          that.

Brian continues to fade, fighting it,
staring at the vast vault in the fabric of
reality ahead.

He tries to speak, but it is hard forming
words now.

                    BRIAN
          Nick -- I just wanted to
          say -- thank you.

Nick smiles and gives his hand a squeeze.

                    NICK
          You`re welcome, mate.
          It`s been a flight to
          remember. Even without
          the movie and the free
          mimosas.

Brian looked back into the rip. A river of
gorgeous colors flow into it now.

They spiral and mix in a glorious array of
shades and tones.

                    BRIAN
          It`s sooo beautifulll --

His head slumps forward on his chest. Nick
leans forward, staring out the window.
Ahead, the rip approaches.

His hand drops to the rheostat that

controls the cabin pressure.

He murmurs to himself, his voice muffled under the oxygen mask.

> NICK
> You`re right, Brian. It
> is beautiful. And why
> not? This is the place
> where life -- all life,
> maybe -- begins. The
> cradle of creation and
> the wellspring of life.
> No Langoliers allowed
> beyond this point.

Colors run across his cheeks and brow in a fountain-spray of hues: jungle green is overthrown by lava orange only to be replaced by yellow-white tropical sunshine which in turn is supplanted by the chilly blue of Northern oceans. He looks up. The rip looms directly ahead. The sound of the jets is lost entirely in a new sound; the 767 seems to be rushing through a wind tunnel filled with feathers.

EXT. PLANE - DAY

Suddenly, directly ahead of the airliner`s nose, a vast nova of light explodes like a heavenly firework.

INT. COCKPIT - DAY

Nick rears back as colors no man has ever imagined flash across his face.

He cries out as Flight 29 rushes into the rip and he twists the cabin-pressure rheostat back up to full.

                    NICK
          Oh, my God, SO BEAUTIFUL!

A split second later the fillings from Nick`s teeth patter onto the cockpit floor. There is a small thump as his watch joins them. Above them, the seat is empty, the still buckled seat belt suddenly flat and empty. Nick Hopewell has ceased to exist.

EXT. PLANE -LATER THAT NIGHT

Time has passed and night has fallen once more as the plane drones through the air. The rip is no longer in evidence, either left far behind or disappeared entirely.

INT. COCKPIT - NIGHT

Brian`s eyelids flutter and he groans, shaking his head as he slowly returns to consciousness. He lifts a hand to his nose only to realize he has bleed from the depressurization. He pulls his handkerchief, wiping at it as he checks his control board. They`re right where he wants them to be. He flicks on the radio, speaking into his headset.

                    BRIAN
          LAX ground control, this
          is American Pride Flight
          29, repeat, two-niner.

                    BRIAN (CONT.)
              Mayday, ground control, I
              am declaring an emergency
              here --

Laurel appears in the doorway behind him,
her face slack, her eyes dead, watching
him.

                    LAUREL
              Oh, quit it. Just quit
              it.

Brian whirls to look at her.

                    BRIAN
              Sit <u>down</u>, dammit! We`re
              coming into heavy traffic
              unannounced

Laurel cuts him off as she steps up to the
cockpit window, looking out.

                    LAUREL
              There`s no heavy traffic
              down there. Look for
              yourself. We`re over L.A.
              all right, but what do
              you see out the windows?
              I`ll tell you <u>nothing</u>!
              <u>Nothing at all</u>!

Brian glances out the window. Laurel is
right. There is nothing to be seen out
there but the city landscape below, not
a thing moving, bathed in total complete
darkness.

EXT. LOS ANGELES - NIGHT

Flight 29 cruises slowly above the ground sixteen miles east of LAX. Below, the city skyline is etched in moonlight, but all is silent, dark, and motionless. The plane`s belly slides open. The undercarriage drops down and spreads out. The landing gear locks into place. The American Pride jet begins it descent, banking slightly to the right as it comes down the chute toward the darkened airport and runways that are LAX.

INT. COCKPIT - NIGHT

Brian corrects course visually, glancing down at they pass over a cluster of darkened airport motels, then the enormous airport itself. Laurel sits beside him, strapped into her seat, her gaze vacant and defeated.

EXT. PLANE - NIGHT

The plane shoots in toward the runway, passing over a short strip of dead grass, and then the concrete is unrolling thirty feet below. The huge jet engines suddenly start to cough and miss.

INT. COCKPIT - NIGHT

Brian glances at his fuel indicators. They read ZERO. He pushes forward on the yoke, bringing the plane in hard.

EXT. PLANE - NIGHT

It hits the runway with a thump, bounces up and comes down even harder.

INT. COCKPIT - NIGHT

Brian and Laurel are slammed forward in their seats. Their chest harnesses lock. Laurel cries out. Brian brings the flaps up and hits the reverse thrusters, shoving them full open.

EXT. RUNWAY - NIGHT

The plane, moving at over a hundred miles an hour, begins to slow. The thrusters suddenly start to flame and gutter out.

INT. COCKPIT - NIGHT

A warning buzzer sounds and red ENGINE SHUTDOWN lights flash on. Brian grabs the intercom.

                    BRIAN
          Hang on! We`re going in
          hard!

Brian fights the yoke as thrusters two and four cut out on the control board.

INT. MAIN CABIN - NIGHT

Rudy hangs on to his rosary, Bob hangs on to his seat, and Albert and Bethany hang on to each other.

EXT. RUNWAY - NIGHT

Flight 29 races down the runway in ghostly silence, with only the flaps and brakes to slow her now.

INT. COCKPIT - NIGHT

Brian fights the yoke, staring out the window helplessly as the concrete runway runs away beneath the plane and the criss-cross tangle of taxiways looms ahead. And suddenly, dead ahead, sits the carcass of a Pacific Airways commuter jet.

EXT. RUNWAY - NIGHT

The 767 rushes toward the commuter jet, still doing an easy sixty-five miles an hour.

INT. COCKPIT - NIGHT

Brian horses the 767 to the right, leaning into the dead steering yolk with every ounce of his strength.

EXT. RUNWAY - NIGHT

The plane responds soggily and skates by the parked jet with only six feet to spare. Its windows flash past like a row of blind eyes. Then they are rolling at thirty-five miles an hour and still slowing toward the United terminal, where at least a dozen planes are parked at extended jet ways.

INT. COCKPIT - NIGHT

Brian glances up, sees the United terminal looming ahead, and leans back in his seat, slamming down on the foot brakes.

EXT. RUNWAY - NIGHT

The plane still moves forward, but its speed is slowly decreasing.

INT. COCKPIT - NIGHT

Brian braces himself against the back of the seat, pushing down with all his strength on the brakes.

EXT. UNITED TERMINAL - NIGHT

American Pride Flight 29 rolls to a halt just a foot from crashing into Gate 29 of the United Airlines terminal.

INT. COCKPIT - NIGHT

Brian lets off the brakes, slumping in his seat with an exhausted sigh. He flicks all the switches on the control panel off, then turns to check on Laurel.

                    BRIAN
          That was about as close
          as I`d ever want to cut
          it.

She looks at him with dull, apathetic
eyes. Blood leaks from her nose.

                    LAUREL
          You should have let us
          crash. Everything we
          tried -- Dinah - Nick
          -- all for nothing. It`s
          just the same here. Just
          the same.

Brian unbuckles his harness and gets
unsteadily to his feet. He takes his
handkerchief out of his pocket and hands
it to her.

                    BRIAN
          Wipe your nose. It`s
          bleeding.

She takes the handkerchief as he slips out
the door.

INT. MAIN CABIN - NIGHT

Brian appears in the main cabin, stopping
by the bulkhead and counting noses.
Bethany`s head is pressed against Albert`s
chest and she is sobbing hard.

Rudy unbuckles his seat belt and stands
up, rapping his head on the overhead

compartment.

Bob sits in his seat, staring quietly at
Brian. Brian looks at all of them as Laurel
appears behind him.

                    BRIAN
          Let`s get off the plane.
          Only this time we use the
          cockpit exit.

He turns back for the cockpit. Laurel and
the others follow.

ACT 7

EXT. PLANE - NIGHT

Brian slides down a metal ladder extended from a trapdoor beneath the cockpit to join the others on the tarmac. They stand there for a moment, looking around at this new world. A light wind ruffles their hair. Bethany cocks an ear. She hears a LOW HUM, a one note sustain that seems to go on and on.

> BETHANY
>
> What`s that -- that humming? It sounds like electricity.

> BOB
>
> No, it doesn`t. It sounds like --

He falls silent as he tries to name the sound and fails. Brian tilts his head, listening.

> BRIAN
>
> It doesn`t sound like anything I`ve ever heard before.
> (a beat, then)
> Well, at least the jet way service door is open.

He steps out from behind the 767`s nose and points toward the elevated doors. The

force of their arrival at Gate 29 has
knocked the rolling ladder away. They walk
toward it. Brian glances at Albert.

                    BRIAN
          Help me with the ladder

Bob suddenly jerks to a halt, raising a
hand.

                     BOB
             Wait!

They freeze. Brian looks at Bob. The older
man stands there, looking around with
cautious wonder.

                    BRIAN
          What? What is it, Bob?
          What do you see?

                     BOB
          Just another deserted
          airport. But it`s what I
          feel.

He raises a hand to his cheek -- them
simply holds it out in the air like a man
trying to flag a ride.

Brian starts to ask what he means and
then realizes he already knows. He murmurs
aloud.

                    BRIAN
            It`s a breeze. The air is
            in <u>motion</u>.

                    ALBERT
          Holy cow.

He pops a finger in his mouth and holds it
up. An unbelieving grin touches his face.
Laurel breaks in. A grin is beginning to
tug at her mouth also.

                    LAUREL
          That isn`t all either.
          Listen!

She dashes toward the wing of the 767,
then back to them, her hair streaming out
behind her. Her high heels click crisply
on the concrete. She looks at the others
happily.

                    LAUREL
          Did you hear it? Did you
          <u>hear</u> it?

They all heard. The flat muffled quality is
gone. Bethany raises her hands and rapidly
claps out the back beat of an old Routers
instrumental, "Let`s Go." Each clap is as
clean and clear as a gunshot. A delighted
grin spreads over her face. Rudy looks at
the others.

                    RUDY
          What does it mean? If
          things have really gone
          back to normal, where`s
          the electricity? Where
          are the <u>people</u>?

                    ALBERT
          And what`s that noise?
          It`s getting closer.

They all stop, listening. The HUMMING
SOUND <u>is</u> closer, louder. It sounds like
a wind blowing across an open pipe, or
an inhuman choir uttering the same open-
throated syllable in unison: <u>aaaaaa</u> --.
Bob shakes his head.

                     BOB
          I don`t know. Let`s push
          the ladder back into
          position and go into the
          --

Laurel grabs his shoulder. Her voice is
tense and strained.

                    LAUREL
          You know something! I can
          see that you do. Let the
          rest of us in on it.

He hesitates for a moment, then shakes his
head.

                     BOB
          I want to go inside and
          look around first.

Brian and Albert turn, pushing the ladder
back into place.

The others start to ascend it, the two of
them following.

INT. BOARDING LOBBY - NIGHT

They come through a jet way door to find themselves in a large, round room with boarding gates located at intervals along the single curving wall. The rows of seats stand ghostly and deserted; the overhead fluorescents are dark squares. From outside the choral humming continues to swell, approaching like a slow invisible wave: -- aaaaaaaaaaaaaaa! Bob turns to the others.

                    BOB
          Come with me. Quickly,
          please.

He sets off toward the concourse and the others fall into line behind him.

INT. CONCOURSE - NIGHT

They enter the long hallway, their heels clicking brightly past dim, dark advertising posters on the walls: Watch CNN, Smoke Marlboros, Drive Hertz, Read Newsweek. See Disneyland. And that open-throated choral humming continues to grow around them. They reach a cafeteria-style restaurant, and Bob leads them inside.

INT. CAFETERIA - NIGHT

Without pausing, Bob goes around the counter and takes a pastry from a pile sitting there. He tries to open it with his teeth, but can`t quite manage. He makes a

small, disgusted sound, and tosses it over
the counter to Albert.

                    BOB
          You do it. Quickly,
          Albert! Quickly!

Albert tears open the cellophane, takes
out the pastry, and bites into it. Cream
and raspberry jam squirt out the sides.
Albert grins, looking up at them all with
a full mouth.

                  ALBERT
          It`s delicious! <u>Delicious</u>!

He offers it to Bethany who takes an even
bigger bite. Laurel suddenly laughs,
beginning to feel a lot better. The
choral sound continues to swell, a sound
with no direction at all, a sourceless,
singing sigh that exists all around them:
- <u>AAAAAAAAA</u>! Bob suddenly races around
the counter, jostling the condiment tray.
It falls over with a gorgeous, resounding
crash, spraying plastic cutlery and little
packets of mustard, ketchup, and relish
everywhere. He yells over his shoulder as
he hurries for the door.

                    BOB
          Quickly! It`s going to
          happen any second, and
          we can`t be here when it
          does! I don`t think it`s
          safe!

                    BETHANY
            What isn`t safe?

She never gets a chance to finish because
Albert puts his arm around her shoulder
and hustles her after Bob and the others
who have already bolted toward the doors.

INT. CONCOURSE - NIGHT

They dash back along the concourse for the
boarding lobby. Now the echoing rattle of
their footfalls is almost totally lost in
the POWERFUL HUM which fills the deserted
terminal, echoing and re-echoing through
the spoked corridors.

INT. BOARDING LOUNGE - DAY

They dash into the lobby and skid to a
halt. They see an ethereal light begin
to skate over the empty chairs, the dark
ARRIVALS and DEPARTURES TV monitors, and
the boarding desks. Red follows blue;
yellow follows red; green follows yellow.
They all stand there, staring, filled with
the clear assurance that they are on the
verge of something, <u>some great and amazing
thing</u>.

                     BOB
            Over here!

He leads them toward the wall beside the
jet way through which they had entered.
This is a passengers only area, guarded by
a red velvet rope. Bob jumps it as easily

as the high-school hurdler he must once
have been.

                    BOB
          Against the wall!

The others join him, pressing against the
wall like suspects in a police line-up.
In the deserted circular lounge that now
lays before them, the color flares for a
moment, bathing their faces in its glow
-- and then begins to circle the room even
faster.

The SOUND continues to deepen and become more
real. VOICES can now be heard, footsteps,
yells, even babies crying. Laurel yells
out, half-weeping, half laughing.

                   LAUREL
          I don`t know what it is,
          but it`s <u>wonderful</u>! I
          love it!

Bob yells above the growing hum which now
seems to be splintering into many different
sounds, more and more of them recognizable
even in the jumble.

                    BOB
          I hope we`re safe here. I
          think we will be. We`re
          out of the main traffic
          area.

                   BRIAN
          What`s going to happen?

                    BOB
When we went through the
time-rip headed east, we
traveled back in time!
We went into the past!
Perhaps as little as
fifteen minutes -- do you
remember me telling you
that?

Brian nods and Albert`s face suddenly lights
up. He yells over the growing cacophony
of noises, a million different sounds
in there now, people talking, laughing,
departure and arrival announcements over
the PA system, feet scuffling, the sounds
of life!

                    ALBERT
This time it brought us
into the future! That`s
it, isn`t it? This time
rip brought us into the
future!

                    BOB
I believe so, yes! And
instead of arriving in
a dead world -- a world
which had moved on without
us -- we have arrived in
a world waiting to be
born! I believe that the
present is on the verge
of catching up to us.

The colors continue to race faster and

faster as the deep, reverberating quality of the hum suddenly drops and the voices within it grow louder, clearer. Whole words, even phrases are suddenly heard, coming out of the empty air in front of the small band.

                    WOMAN (V.O.)
               -- I have to call her
          before she decides

                    MAN (V.O.)
          I really don`t think that
          option is viable --

Then one passes directly before them in the emptiness on the other side of the velvet rope.

                    ANOTHER MAN (V.O.)
               -- home and dry if
          we can just turn this
          thing over to the parent
          company

Brian Engle grins and takes Laurel`s hand. Beside them, Albert suddenly hugs Bethany, and she begins to shower kisses all over his face. Bob and Rudy grin at each other delightedly. Overhead, the fluorescent squares in the ceiling begin to flash on. They go sequentially, racing out from the center of the room in an expanding circle of light that flows down the concourse, chasing the night-shadows like a flock of black sheep.

For a long moment the wide circle of the boarding lounge remains deserted, a place haunted by the voices and footsteps of the not-quite-living. Bob presses himself back against the wall with a murmur.

                    BOB
          Brace yourselves. There
          may be a jerk.

A bare second later, all of them feel a thud as though the moving present has caught up with this world of the future and pulled it along. They all rock forward, unsteady on their feet. Albert grabs Rudy to keep him from falling over. A huge, gooney smile splits his face. Laurel gasps and points at the lounge ahead of them.

                  LAUREL
          Look! Oh, Brian -- look!

They all look and feel their breath stop. The boarding lounge is suddenly full of ghosts. Ethereal, transparent figures cross and criss-cross the large central area; men in business suits toting briefcases, women in smart traveling dresses, teenagers in Levi`s and tee-shirts with rock group logos. Brian`s eyes widen as a ghost-father leads two small ghost children past, and through them he can see more ghosts sitting in the chairs, reading transparent copies of <u>Cosmopolitan</u>, <u>Esquire</u>, and <u>U.S. News and World Report</u>. Then the color suddenly solidifies above the ghostly figures and dives into them in a series of cometary flickers, solidifying them, and the echoing voices resolve themselves into the prosaic stereo swarm of real human voices.

The two children are the only ones who happen to be looking directly at the survivors of Flight 29 when the change takes place; they are the only ones who see four men and two women appear in a place where there had only been a wall the second before. The little boy shouts, tugging at his father`s right hand.

                    LITTLE BOY
          Daddy!

The little girl joins in, tugging at his left.

                    LITTLE GIRL
          Dad!

The father stops, tossing them an impatient glance.

                    FATHER
          What? I`m looking for
          your mother!

The little girl points at Brian and his bedraggled quintet of passengers.

                    LITTLE GIRL
          New people! Look at the
          new people!

The man glances at Brian and the others.

His mouth tightens nervously. It`s the
dried blood on their faces and clothes.

Brian, Laurel, and Bethany have all
suffered nosebleeds.

The man tightens his grip on his children`s
hands and pulls them away fast.

                    FATHER
          Yes, great. Now help me
          look for your mother.

Then they are gone into the hurrying crowd.
Laurel turns to Brian.

Tears stream down her face and she makes
no effort to wipe them away.

                    LAUREL
          Did you hear her? Did you
          hear what that little
          girl said?

                    BRIAN
          Yes.

                    LAUREL
          Is that what we are,
          Brian? The new people? Do
          you think that`s what we
          are?

                    BRIAN
          I don`t know, but that`s
          what it feels like.

                    ALBERT
          That was wonderful. My
          God, that was the most
          wonderful thing.

Bethany yells out happily, beginning to
clap out "Let`s Go," again.

                    BETHANY
          <u>Totally tubular</u>!

                    BOB
          What do we do now, Brian?
          Any ideas?

Brian glances around at the choked boarding
area and turns back to the others.

                    BRIAN
          I want to go outside.
          Breathe some fresh air.
          And look at the sky.

                    BOB
          Shouldn`t we inform the
          authorities of what --

                    BRIAN
          We will. But the sky
          first.

Rudy suddenly grins at him, asking him
hopefully.

                    RUDY
          And maybe something to
          eat on the way?

Brian laughs.

BRIAN

Why not?

Bethany glances down at her wristwatch and breaks in.

BETHANY

My watch has stopped.

Brian glances at his. So do the others. All their watches have stopped.

Brian takes his off and drops it indifferently to the ground.

BRIAN

Let`s blow this joint.
Unless any of you want to
wait for the next flight
east.

LAUREL

Not today, but soon.
All the way to England.
There`s a man I have to
see in Fluting. The old
folks still call him the
gaffer.

ALBERT

What are you talking
about?

Laurel laughs with a smile.

349

                    LAUREL
          Daisies. I`m talking
          about daisies. Come on
          -let`s go.

Bob grins widely.

                     BOB
          As for me, I think the
          next time I have to go
          to Boston, I`ll take the
          train.

Laurel toes Brian`s watch, throwing him a
glance.

                    LAUREL
          Are you sure you don`t
          want that? It looks
          expensive.

Brian grins and shakes his head.

                    BRIAN
          Not at all. I know what
          time it is.

                    LAUREL
          Oh? And what time is
          that?

                    BRIAN
          It`s half past now.

Albert claps him on the back and they leave
the boarding lounge in a group, weaving
their way through the clots of passengers

into the concourse.

INT. CONCOURSE - NIGHT

The little group walks happily down the concourse. A good many of the passengers they pass stop and look curiously after them, and not just because some of them appear to have recently suffered nosebleeds, or because they are laughing their way down the concourse.

They look because the six people seem to be somehow <u>brighter</u> than anyone else in the crowded walkway. More actual. More <u>there</u>.

Brian suddenly leaps forward, joyously sweeping Laurel into a run down the concourse. She laughs and hugs him as the six of them run toward the escalators and the outside world beyond.

THE END